Topaz

on Ice

WE SPARKLE WHATEVER

*Read all about Topaz's first year
at Precious Gems:*

First term: Topaz Steals the Show
Second term: Topaz Takes a Chance
Third term: Topaz in the Limelight

Summer holidays: Topaz Takes a Break

And Topaz's second year:

First term: Topaz on Ice
Second term: Topaz Takes the Stage

More titles from Hodder Children's Books:

Thora
Gillian Johnson

Otto and the Flying Twins
Otto and the Bird Charmers
Charlotte Haptie

Topaz
on Ice

HELEN BAILEY

Illustrated by Bill Dare

Hodder
Children's
Books

A division of Hodder Headline Limited

For Hannah Boehm.

Chapter One

'Did *we* look like that?' asked Topaz, as she watched the first-years walk through the front door of Precious Gems Stage School and stand, bewildered, in the entrance hall. 'They look terrified!'

'I'm sure I did,' admitted Sapphire. 'I remember everyone staring at me because Mum's an actress. It's not even as if I wanted to go to stage school!'

Seeing the first-years stand uncomfortably in their stiff new uniform, Topaz remembered how out of place she'd felt this time last year, turning up in a boy's second-hand blazer, which, being maroon, wasn't even quite the right colour.

Thank goodness Mum found the money for a proper one, she thought, stroking the sleeve of her new claret blazer. *I couldn't be a second-year in the wrong blazer!*

As pupils came to Precious Gems from far and wide, many hadn't seen each other over the long holidays, and there was lots of hugging, giggling and chattering as the corridor became packed with excited faces, everyone trying to catch up on all the gossip in the few minutes before the first school assembly.

A bright-red head bobbed down the corridor, plaits flying.

'Not playing the piano in assembly?' asked Sapphire as Ruby Ruddle emerged through the crowd, smiling and waving.

'No, thank goodness,' said Ruby, who suffered from crippling stage fright. 'If I'd had to perform on the first day back it would have ruined the holidays.'

'Did you drop your bags in the East Wing?' asked Topaz, hugging her friend. She'd seen Ruby and Sapphire in the holidays but it wasn't the same as seeing each other every day. Ruby lived in Sutton Perry, too far to travel into Starbridge each day, so she boarded in the East Wing during the week.

Ruby nodded. 'Dad brought me in early this morning. I couldn't *wait* to see you. He said that to thank you for taking me on holiday to Whoosh Waterworld he'd like to invite us all to the Ice Spectacular show in Sutton Perry at the end of term!'

Topaz's eyes lit up. 'Fantastic. Will you thank him for me?'

'And me,' said Sapphire. 'I've seen the Ice Spectacular once. It was like watching a ballet on ice.'

Ruby pushed her glasses up her nose and peered at the terrified first-years, now huddled together, clutching their bags as if clinging on to them for safety. She shot Topaz a puzzled look.

'Shouldn't you be over there with them, instead of gossiping with us over here?' she asked.

For a moment Topaz looked blank. Then with horror she remembered what she was supposed to be doing. At the end of last term, Miss Diamond had asked her to look after the new pupils on their first day, but in the excitement of going back to school and seeing her friends, she had completely forgotten! Before she could reach them, a bell sounded and a sea of claret blazers flowed down the corridor. Like lemmings, the first-years followed the older pupils through the open door and into the school hall.

I'd better get out of assembly as soon as it finishes and make sure they don't wander off, thought Topaz, rushing after them.

In the school hall dust swirled under the lights, and even though the school kitchens had been closed for the holidays, the smell of stinky school dinners still hung in the air. At the far end of the room, thick velvet curtains framed a small stage, their crimson folds held back by gold rope. Gloria Gold, the music mistress, darted into the orchestra pit below the stage, ready to play the piano. The doors to the hall creaked shut, and Miss Adelaide Diamond, Headmistress of Precious Gems Stage School, strode on to the stage, the beads around her large chest gently rising and falling, the fabric of her dress billowing around her. It didn't matter how many times the pupils saw her make an entrance, whether into a classroom or on to a stage, they all agreed it was obvious why their Headmistress was the *only* actress *ever* to win five Golden Nugget Awards. Old, grey and wrinkled off stage, on it, Miss Diamond was every inch the star.

'Welcome!' she boomed in her crystal-clear voice. 'Welcome back, old pupils, and a *very* warm welcome to our new intake of first-years!'

The school clapped and cheered. Miss Diamond waited for the applause to die down.

'As a change, Miss Gold suggested we sing a song for this first assembly. Years Two and upwards all know it well as it's part of the first-year curriculum. For the new pupils, please refer to the

4

song sheet you will have been given. The song is appropriately titled, "Welcome!"'

Topaz's stomach lurched. It must have been *her* job to give out the song sheets!

From the orchestra pit, Gloria Gold began to thump out the introduction on the piano. Topaz looked around her. The older pupils were standing straight, heads up, shoulders back, smiles on their faces, ready to launch into the song. The first-years, on the other hand, were looking puzzled. The music mistress had composed the song as practice for breathing techniques and scales. There was no way the new pupils would even be able to guess the words.

The song came to a rousing end, and Miss Diamond began to run through a list of school notices, staff changes and school rules. Topaz was listening carefully, not because she was the slightest bit interested that there was a new history teacher called Mrs Hornblende, or that a new floor had been laid in the dance studio during the holidays, but so that the *moment* assembly ended, she could dart out of the school hall, into the corridor and start being a chaperone.

'And when you are too tired to dance another step, sing another note or deliver another line, remember the school motto: *We Sparkle Whatever the Occasion.* In other words, the show *must* go on!'

To a round of applause, Miss Diamond descended

the steps at the side of the stage and began to make her way through the crowd of pupils, who parted as she swept towards the door.

'Excuse me!' hissed Topaz, pushing through the crowd. 'Let me through!'

But as she tried to scurry to the end of the row, she stumbled over a large bag resting at the feet of one of the first-years. As if in slow motion, Topaz flew up in the air, dived down to the ground, skidded along the floor on her elbows, and stopped, spread-eagled, at the feet of a startled Adelaide Diamond.

'Ah, Topaz,' said the Headmistress, quickly regaining her composure. 'Welcome back. How nice to see you. Are you hurt?'

A ripple of giggles rang round the hall.

Topaz scrambled to her feet. Her pride was hurt more than her body.

'I'm fine,' she said, brushing dust off her blazer. 'Sorry, Miss Diamond.'

The Headmistress gave Topaz a sharp look. 'We'll talk later,' she said, continuing to sweep towards the door.

'Are you OK?' Sapphire and Ruby rushed to see whether their friend was hurt.

'I'm fine!' Topaz said. 'I'll see you in geography later!'

'But, Topaz! What about your blazer?' Ruby called out as Topaz raced off in hot pursuit of the first-years.

'I guess she'll find out soon enough,' said Sapphire, as they watched their friend become swallowed up in the crowd.

Topaz felt *very* important.

'First-years gather round!' she called out. 'Quickly! Quickly!'

Twenty first-years clustered around her. Topaz looked at their eager faces and realized that she could say *anything* to them and they would be impressed. She remembered being very impressed when her chaperone, Pearl Wong, told them she'd been in a Speedy Snax TV advert. Now it was her turn to impress.

'Hi! I'm Topaz L'Amour and I'm a second-year pupil. I'll be looking after you today. Last year I appeared in *lots* of professional productions.'

A dark-haired girl with olive skin fixed her large green eyes on Topaz.

'You're a second-year, right?'

Topaz nodded and gave a slightly smug smile.

'But I thought first-years weren't allowed to take professional engagements, so how come you did?'

'Sometimes they make exceptions,' said Topaz, beginning to lead her flock down the corridor and up the stairs, accompanied by the sound of squeaky new shoes. 'I was an exception.'

'So it's a rule that can be broken,' the girl persisted. 'I'm thinking of getting an agent straight away. I'm quite well known on the junior entertainment circuit. You might have heard of me. Amber Morelli?'

The dark-haired girl was starting to irritate Topaz, so she ignored her and pointed to the first-year locker room. 'Put everything in your lockers and don't forget your key,' she announced as the first-years poured into the room, eager to get rid of their heavy bags. Being at stage school meant you had to have so many things. Tap-shoes, ballet-shoes, character shoes, leotards in different colours, skirts in different colours *and* different lengths. The list went on and on.

Topaz followed them in and spotted the pile of song sheets sitting on a bench, next to a clipboard. She briefly thought about hiding them, but decided against it. She *had* to be a perfect pupil; Miss Diamond had made it quite clear that if she got into any more trouble, her scholarship would be withdrawn at the end of the term. Leaving Precious Gems would mean she'd have to go to her local school,

Starbridge High, and face the taunts of school bully Kylie Slate and the sympathy of her old best friend Janice Stone. Topaz imagined Kylie calling her a sad loser. And what about her name? Kylie and Janice knew her as Topaz Love, but Topaz had changed her surname to L'Amour when she'd gone to stage school as she thought it sounded more glamorous. Would she have to go back to using plain old Topaz Love? She shuddered at the thought.

This term I'm not going to tell any *fibs, get into* any *trouble or do* anything *I'm not supposed to,* she thought. *This term I'm going to be Miss Perfect!*

Topaz became aware that the sound of large bags being forced into small spaces and the banging of metal doors had finished, and everyone was staring at her, wondering what to do next. After she had ticked names off the list attached to the clipboard she announced, 'Time for a tour of the school! Follow me.'

Topaz led the first-years through the maze of corridors and rooms which made up Precious Gems. Originally two large houses knocked into one in Stellar Terrace, East Starbridge, the school had gradually expanded with a series of extensions and alterations until it was a jumble of corridors, classrooms and dance studios. Topaz had never got used to sitting studying equations whilst above her she could hear the thud of pupils practising their jetés in ballet, or trying to concentrate on history to the sound of scales being sung over and over again. To her, academic lessons were a waste of time, and hearing others perform whilst she studied was torture. But as Miss Diamond kept reminding her, Precious Gems placed as much importance on schoolwork as it did on stage work.

Topaz stopped outside one of the dance studios.

'You'll spend the next couple of days being graded and then you'll be put into classes depending on how good you are at singing and dancing and—'

'I'm good!' Amber Morelli piped up. 'Everyone says so *and* I have show business experience so I won't need to be graded.'

'Oh yes you will!' Topaz glared at the pushy first-year. 'How do you know the others aren't better than you?'

Some of the first-years forgot their nerves and sniggered. Amber Morelli looked put out.

'*I've* got a scholarship,' she pouted. 'So I must be good.'

Topaz looked the new pupil straight in the eyes and said in what she hoped was a very withering tone, '*So* have I.'

Amber's green eyes glowed with mock pity. 'Yes, but mine's because I'm talented, *not* because we couldn't afford the fees.'

Topaz was about to explode with rage when one of the other pupils said softly, 'We couldn't help but notice your blazer.'

For a split second, Topaz was taken back to her first day at Precious Gems, when she had arrived in the hideous hand-me-down, but then she remembered she was wearing a brand-new one.

'What about my blazer?' she demanded.

The pupils around her looked embarrassed and began to stare at the floor and shuffle their feet. All except Amber Morelli who piped up, 'From the look of the worn elbows, it's obviously second-hand!'

Topaz sat in the second-year locker room and looked in despair at the brand-new blazer draped across her knees. Skidding on the floor in assembly had split both sleeves at the elbows, and the tear ran up to the shoulders and almost down to both wrists. Even the silky crimson lining had ripped. The claret wool was covered in a ghostly white layer of dust and the powdery white resin the dancers used to stop themselves slipping. Her first day of the second year, and *already* things had gone wrong. She knew her mother, Lola, had done double shifts at Happy Al's Café so that they could afford a new pair of tap-shoes *and* a new blazer. Topaz had felt so good when she'd tried it on in the school outfitter's and the shop assistant had purred, 'The claret of Precious Gems is such a beautiful colour.' Now it was ruined.

If only *I'd met the first-years earlier and they'd put their*

11

bags in their lockers, thought Topaz, close to tears. *Then I wouldn't have tripped over. The first day of the first term of the second year and* already *it's turning into a disastrophe!*

A disastrophe was the worst possible disaster on Topaz's three-level disaster scale. The 3D-scale took into account not only the actual disaster, but the consequences of the disaster. A small disaster, nothing more than a minor annoyance, was a disasterette. A straightforward disaster was a major problem, but without any long-term consequences. But if there was a disaster which had long-term catastrophic consequences for the rest of Topaz's life, then *that* was a disastrophe.

Take forgetting to show the new pupils to their lockers so they had to take their bags into assembly.

If the first-years had taken their bags into assembly and just cluttered up the aisles so that other first-years had to step over them, it wouldn't matter. This wouldn't even be classed as a disasterette. But one of them might trip over a bag and fall down, twisting their ankle or hitting their head, and Topaz would be in *big* trouble for not looking after them. *That* would be a disaster. But a disaster could easily become a full-scale disastrophe. Suppose it wasn't a first-year that was injured? What if, instead of just falling over the bag and ripping her blazer, Topaz had broken her ankle?

She would have to miss dance classes for weeks, perhaps an entire term. She'd fall so far behind, Miss Diamond would insist she went to after-school dance classes with the dreaded PTs, the part-timers from other schools who paid for lessons at Precious Gems. Everyone in her year would be better than her, they'd start pointe work in ballet before her and she'd *never* catch up, *ever*! Perhaps she'd even have to drop back down to first-year dance classes! Forgetting to see the first-years to their lockers could definitely have been a disastrophe.

But I didn't break my ankle and I'll get another blazer somehow, thought Topaz, getting up and stuffing her mangled blazer into her locker. *I'll prove to everyone that I can be a perfect pupil, starting from now.*

Chapter Two

Bob Feldspar, the geography teacher, stood at the front of the class writing a lesson plan on the board. He felt like bolting for the door. It wasn't only the pupils who found it hard to come back to school after a long holiday. Teachers did too. The days were no longer your own to do as you wanted. Timetables told you what you should be doing and ringing bells signalled when to do it. There was homework to mark, reports to write and lessons to plan. It didn't help that the pupils at Precious Gems regarded him as the enemy. At the end of last term, he'd thought about applying for a job at another school, one where pupils would enjoy learning and look forward to his lessons, but he'd been so exhausted, he couldn't even bring himself to pick up a pen to fill out the application form. So here he was again, back at Precious Gems, trying to teach a class of wannabe stars about rock formations and continents.

He turned away from the board to face the class and had such a shock, he nearly jumped out of his corduroy trousers. Sitting in the front row, wide-eyed and eager, was Topaz L'Amour. He'd been *sure* Adelaide Diamond wasn't going to offer the girl a second-year scholarship, particularly in view of the appalling end-of-year report he'd given her. He knew some of the other academic staff felt the same, especially the science teacher, Trudi Tuffstone, who still found it hard to have Topaz and a Bunsen burner in the same room without getting the shakes.

I'll go straight to the Headmistress after class and find out what's going on, he thought to himself.

It unnerved him that Topaz was sitting at the front of the class. Usually she hung around outside the door, waiting to come in at the last possible moment, or sat at the back flicking through a magazine. What *was* she up to?

Bob Feldspar cleared his throat. 'So you're all still here,' he said, looking around the class as if a bad smell had wafted under his nose. 'As none of you became famous film stars over the holiday you still need to learn about geography.' He gave a sarcastic chuckle.

He caught Topaz looking intently at him. 'I'm amazed you're finding this lesson so interesting, Topaz, but I suppose it's because I haven't started teaching yet. There's still time for your eyes to glaze over.'

The class giggled.

'And where is your blazer?' he demanded. 'You know you have to wear your blazer in class!'

Topaz flashed him her best smile. She knew he couldn't stand her and she knew he would do his best to be mean to her, but *this* term, she wasn't going to give him *any* opportunity to fault her.

'I was just thinking what a lovely tie that is, Mr Feldspar,' she said, even though she thought the tie was hideous. 'Is it new?'

Bob Feldspar proudly fingered the purple silk tie dotted with a silver SS logo and smiled. This time it was the class's turn to feel uneasy. Fusty Feldspar rarely smiled.

'It is rather special, isn't it?' he said. 'It was presented to me for twenty-five years' service to the Starbridge Strollers amateur dramatic group. People still talk about my performance as the Pirate King in *Pirates of Penzance*.'

The class fidgeted with embarrassment. It was difficult to

believe that the large ungainly frame of Fusty Feldspar could ever cast aside his corduroy suits and strange Cornish pasty-shaped shoes to become a pirate of the high seas. Topaz found it hard to keep a straight face, but managed to continue to look interested.

'And for fifty years, Mr Feldspar? What do you get for fifty years?'

A dreamy look passed across Bob Feldspar's face. He was thinking of all the new productions he could be involved in over the next twenty-five years. The songs he could sing, the scenery he could paint, the lines he could learn, the leading ladies . . . He suddenly realized twenty pairs of eyes were looking at him with a very odd expression.

'For fifty years the logo is gold instead of silver,' he said sharply. 'Now let's get on with the lesson.'

The class sighed and began to rummage in their pencil cases, as new exercise books were passed around.

Bob Feldspar placed a large globe on his desk.

'As it's the first day back I thought we'd take a look at where some of you went for your holidays.'

Topaz groaned inwardly. Other than the holiday at Whoosh Waterworld with Ruby and Sapphire, she hadn't been anywhere during the break, and it seemed unlikely that the town of Boddington would be marked on the globe.

'Now, I need a volunteer to spin this thing.'

Topaz's hand shot up.

'Please, Mr Feldspar. Can I spin the globe?'

Further back in the class, Ruby and Sapphire exchanged puzzled looks.

Bob Feldspar hesitated. He was surprised and suspicious. Trouble always seemed to follow Topaz around, but the second-year seemed keen. What possible harm could she do with a globe? He looked around the class but there were no other volunteers, just vacant bored faces. He nodded at Topaz who scrambled out of her chair and scooted to the teacher's desk.

It soon became clear that whilst Topaz believed most of her classmates had been on exotic foreign holidays, the majority of them had stayed at home and couldn't point to anywhere on the globe. Bob Feldspar, realizing that his lesson plan was going wrong, began to waffle on about foreign trips he and Mrs Feldspar and all the little Feldspars had done over the years. The class became restless and began to fidget and Topaz was bored. Pretending to be interested in geography and trying to be a perfect pupil was hard work. Behind Fusty Feldspar's back she began to spin the globe faster and faster.

'And one year we hired a camper van and travelled around the southern hemisphere,' Bob Feldspar droned.

I wonder just how fast this thing goes? thought Topaz, giving the globe another almighty spin, just as Bob Feldspar turned and said, 'Let me show you—'

There was a yell as the end of Bob Feldspar's precious tie became caught in the wildly gyrating globe, which carried on spinning up the tie until it stopped, hanging underneath the terrified teacher's chin like a huge multicoloured boil.

Topaz and the class stared in horror as Bob Feldspar tugged on his tie, only to wedge the globe even further under his chin.

'He's choking!' cried Ruby, darting to the front of the class and trying to loosen the tie. 'It's stuck! We're going to have to cut it off!'

Topaz bolted out of the classroom and looked around the empty corridor. She ran into Miss Diamond's office, but there was no sign of the Headmistress. The school office was locked.

Where is everyone? she thought, running to the front of the school and looking down the steps leading to Stellar Terrace, where a gardener was carefully pruning a rose bush with an enormous pair of shears . . .

'Fusty Feldspar will never write a bad report about me again,' said Topaz as the three friends sat in Happy Al's Café after school, drinking hot chocolate. 'I saved his life.'

'Do you think he'll see it like that?' asked Sapphire doubtfully.

'Of course!' Topaz felt confident the teacher would be forever grateful to her. 'He was about to die. He collapsed when I came in.'

'He fainted and hit his head on the desk when he saw you rushing towards him with those shears,' said Ruby. 'He had a lump the size of an egg on his forehead when I saw him being helped into Miss D's office.'

'What a day!' sighed Topaz, leaning back in her chair and loosening her school tie. 'Perhaps if I tell Mum I saved a teacher's life she might not be so annoyed about this.' She waggled her ripped elbows at her friends.

'I never got to ask you, why did it happen?' said Ruby.

Topaz sighed. 'I was too late to show the first-years to their lockers so they had to take their bags into assembly. I tripped over one of them. It was my own fault really.'

'What were the first-years like?' asked Sapphire.

'Boring,' Topaz sniffed. 'Lots of scaredy-looking girls

and a pushy stage-school brat called Amber who reminded me of Octavia Quaver.' She pulled a face at the mention of Octavia Quaver, who was at rival stage school, Rhapsody's Theatre Academy.

'I bet the pushy one didn't have stars in her eyes at the end of the day when she realized how much work she has to do!' Ruby laughed. 'What did she say?'

Topaz looked puzzled. Then, with a sinking feeling in her stomach, she remembered she was supposed to meet the first-years *after* school as well as before.

'Tell Al I'll pay for my hot chocolate later!' she called as she pushed back her chair and ran out of the door.

She raced up Galaxy Street, past Pearl Wong's father's takeaway, the Wok and Spring Roll on the corner, along Stellar Terrace, and bounded up the steps into Precious Gems. Topaz took the stairs two at a time and dashed towards the first-year locker rooms from where she could hear Amber saying, 'What do you think of Zelma Flint as an agent?' Topaz swung into the locker room and saw Amber talking to Miss Diamond, alone. She was all glossy hair, glittering green eyes and white teeth, and Topaz disliked her even more.

'Ah, Topaz!' Miss Diamond looked pointedly at her watch. 'There you are.'

'I, er, got caught up,' said Topaz. 'Sorry.'

'So I see.' Both the Headmistress and the first-year gave her an odd look. 'Amber had a few questions after her first day, and as you were – busy – *I'm* answering them.'

Topaz felt angry with herself. If she'd been around to answer questions, the pushy first-year wouldn't have had Miss D's undivided attention. Who knows what Amber had said! What if she'd asked the Headmistress to bend the rules and allow *her* to go to auditions? What if Miss D had agreed? What if they went up for the same part and Amber was chosen over her? Another disastrophe, and all because she had forgotten to be the first-year chaperone, again.

One day, two disastrophes, thought Topaz. *What a rotten start to the term.*

Topaz gave Amber a thin smile and said, 'I'm here now, so you can ask me anything you like.'

Amber didn't even look at Topaz, but tossed her hair and said in a brittle voice, 'It's OK. I'm done.' She turned to the Headmistress and gushed, 'Thank you, Miss Diamond. I can't tell you how helpful you've been.'

'You're very welcome, Amber,' Miss Diamond said, as the first-year threw her bag over her shoulder and sauntered out of the locker room.

Headmistress and second-year pupil faced each other. Topaz wasn't sure whether she should speak first or wait for Miss Diamond. There was an icy silence before Topaz couldn't bear it any longer and blurted out, 'Is Mr Feldspar all right? I saved his life!'

Miss Diamond raised an eyebrow. That was *not* the story that Bob Feldspar had given her when he'd staggered into her office with a mangled tie around his neck, a huge lump on his head and a wild look in his eye. He'd claimed that Topaz had deliberately tried to strangle him with a spinning globe before attacking him with a pair of garden shears. Adelaide had told the hysterical geography teacher that she was *sure* Topaz hadn't meant to do any of those things, but Bob was adamant that he wouldn't teach Topaz unless a first-aid kit was available at all times and in *every* classroom.

'It's her or me!' he'd gasped.

Adelaide Diamond told him that he'd had a shock, should take a couple of days off, and they'd talk when he got back, so when Topaz asked after him, all the Headmistress said was, 'He's having a few days at home to recover.'

Topaz nodded. 'He was upset about his tie,' she said. 'I'm sorry we couldn't save it.'

Miss Diamond looked stern, and Topaz noticed with some alarm that the beads which dangled around her large chest had begun to rise and fall. One of the first things you learnt at Precious Gems was that the swell of Miss Diamond's chest was an indication of the level of trouble you were in. A heaving chest with clacking beads meant a storm was ahead, and now the beads were beginning to toss about frantically.

'Why did you trip over this morning, Topaz?' Miss Diamond asked, her voice crisp, cold and distant.

'I tripped over a bag,' said Topaz, realizing that she was walking into trouble, but powerless to do anything about it.

'A first-year bag?'

Topaz nodded.

'Which should have been in a first-year locker *before* assembly.'

Topaz nodded again.

'Which wasn't because . . . ?'

'I didn't show the first-years their lockers until after assembly.'

'Because . . . ?'

'Because I forgot,' admitted Topaz sheepishly.

'Which is why Amber and the others were without the lyrics, wasn't it?'

Topaz nodded for a third time, but was now *sure* that Amber had been complaining about her. That first-year definitely needed watching.

'And you forgot, again, after school,' Miss Diamond said. 'Why?'

'I was busy,' said Topaz. 'And I did remember, eventually.'

The Headmistress glared at Topaz. 'You seem to forget a number of important things. I hope you remember your poor school report last term and that you have to work hard in lessons and must not appear in any professional productions. You have one term to prove to me that you deserve another scholarship.'

Topaz nodded and bit her lip. She hated the thought that her rival, Octavia Quaver, would be rushing around Starbridge going to auditions and castings whilst she was stuck in school, but more than that, she hated the thought that she wouldn't be able to perform. A term without performing seemed a wasted term. Still, there was the thought of the Christmas special of *Murder Mile* to look forward to. She'd filmed it last term, without permission from the school, and Topaz was hoping it wouldn't be shown on television until after the school had broken up for the Christmas holidays.

There was a thick silence. Topaz braced herself for Miss Diamond to launch into her usual lecture about disappointing her and the fact that Topaz was talented but needed more commitment to schoolwork, but instead, the Headmistress simply said, 'Sort yourself out, Topaz, or this will be your last term here,' and walked out.

Topaz felt stung by Miss Diamond's comments. She picked up her bag to leave the locker room and, as she did so, caught sight of her reflection in a mirror. She barely recognized herself. Her blazer was covered in dust and dirty marks from where she had fallen on the floor, and the elbows were torn, the crimson silk lining flapping through the holes. Dirty finger marks ran round the collar of her white shirt, and her claret and grey school tie, knotted neatly in the morning, hung like a limp rag. Her hair was more out of her ponytail than in it. But worst of all was the large moustache of chocolate-sprinkled froth drying around her top lip.

Chapter Three

Topaz's mother, Lola, wasn't angry about the ripped blazer – after all, it was an accident – but she was upset.

'On your first day!' she wailed, as she examined the shredded arms. 'I was hoping it would last you a couple of years. You'll have to dig out your old blazer. This one's beyond repair.'

'No!' Topaz almost spat out her mouthful of pasta with shock. 'I am *not* going back to wearing that maroon monstrosity. I'm a second-year now and second-years do *not* wear manky blazers. Anyway, I threw it out. We'll have to buy a new one, somehow.'

Lola Love sat down at the kitchen table and rubbed her eyes. She'd been up early in the morning cleaning offices in West Starbridge, done a shift at Happy Al's Café, cleaned several private houses and was about to go out to clean an office block in East Starbridge. Topaz's scholarship paid for the school fees at Precious Gems, but didn't cover all the other bits and pieces needed for stage school. Money was tight and another blazer, so soon after buying the first, wasn't in the household budget.

'I'm sorry, Topaz,' she said. 'We just can't afford it. I'll take the badge off yours and put it back on Daniel's. It didn't get thrown out. I found it stuffed under your bed when I was Hoovering.'

Topaz banged her fork down on the table. She knew she was behaving badly, but she couldn't help it.

'*I'll* repair it,' she said, grabbing the blazer. 'I am *not* going to school in last year's blazer and that's that.'

Topaz sat on the end of her bed with a needle and cotton and looked at the huge gashes running along the sleeves. She didn't really know where to start.

I just need to join up the edges, she thought, as she jabbed the needle into one side of the thick material and stabbed her finger on the other side, causing her to yelp.

Her mother put her head around the door. 'Everything all right?'

Topaz, sucking the blood oozing from her finger, nodded.

'I've dug out Daniel's blazer just in case,' said Lola, holding up the hated garment and hanging it on the back of the door.

Topaz didn't say anything but started to sew again. It wasn't as easy as she had thought it would be. The needle seemed very thin compared to the thick material, and every so often a knot appeared in the thread out of nowhere, making pulling the cotton through the material impossible. If she tried to unpick the knot it seemed to get tighter and tighter until there was no alternative but to cut the cotton and start again. Every time she thought of giving up she looked at the old blazer hanging on the door and pressed on, until eventually, she finished a sleeve. She held it up to the light. It looked dreadful, as if it had had an operation that had gone *very* wrong. The material puckered and pulled, and every so often, the silky lining poked through as if it were blood oozing through a wound.

Perhaps it will be better on, she thought, trying to wriggle into the blazer. But she had pulled so much material together either side of the tear that the sleeve had become narrow and she could barely squeeze her arm in. With an almighty tug she finally managed to pull the sleeve over her elbow, only to hear a popping noise as, one by one, her stitches broke apart.

Lola put her head round the door again. She had her coat on and was about to leave.

'No good?' she asked, seeing her daughter's distraught face.

'Terrible,' said Topaz, holding out her arm. 'If anything I've made it worse!'

Lola went over and gave Topaz a kiss. 'Don't worry. I'll think of something.'

'Promise me that I won't be wearing the old blazer tomorrow,' pleaded Topaz, glaring at the maroon monstrosity hanging on the door. 'Please, Mum!'

'I'll do my best,' said Lola. 'Leave it on my bed and I'll have a look at it when I get home.'

Topaz stood miserably at the bus stop outside their flat in Andromeda Road and did her best to ignore the strange looks the other passengers were giving her. When she'd seen her Precious Gems blazer hanging in the hall that morning, at first she'd thought her mother had worked a miracle on the damaged sleeves. Then she'd gasped in horror. Knowing that it was ripped beyond repair, Lola's solution had been to replace the torn sleeves on Topaz's new blazer with the sleeves from Daniel's old blazer. Stitched together, the dark maroon sleeves against the brighter claret blazer made it look as if she had dipped her arms in dirt.

'It's only until I think of something else,' Lola had said when Topaz appeared in the kitchen in floods of tears.

She'd stood in front of the mirror and tried folding her arms, wrapping them across her chest, clasping her hands behind her back, but nothing could hide the fact that her blazer looked *very* odd.

Later, when she changed buses, a group of older girls from Precious Gems nudged each other and giggled. Topaz avoided their stares by studying a poster advertising the ice show in Sutton Perry that Professor Ruddle had invited them all to. The girl on the poster was wearing a silver skating dress and a crown made of diamonds, a bright white smile stretched across her face.

I bet she's never suffered the humiliation of wearing a patchwork blazer, thought Topaz bitterly, as the giggling from the girls became louder.

Topaz sat at the back of the history class and doodled on her exercise book whilst she thought about how to get round the blazer problem. She felt *terrible* being so mean to her mum when she knew her mum tried to do her best for them both. If only there was a way to get her hands on enough money for a new blazer.

Suddenly, she had a thought. Zelma Flint! Zelma was supposed to be her agent but hadn't paid her for her appearance in *Murder Mile*! She'd played two parts, so surely she'd get double the money? Zelma had always got out of paying before, but this time, Topaz wasn't going to wait for Zelma to contact her. It was time to pay her a visit.

Topaz ripped a piece of paper from her exercise book, scribbled: *Can u come in2 town with me?* and folded the note into a paper aeroplane. As she launched the note towards Ruby, Ruby tried to catch it but missed, and, caught on a breeze from an open window, the paper plane flew towards the history teacher, Mrs Hornblende, and crash-landed on her head.

The class giggled and Ruby blushed crimson as the teacher pulled the note from her hair, unfolded it and read it.

'I don't allow pupils to organize their social lives during my lessons,' Mrs Hornblende roared at Ruby. 'Perhaps staying behind after school for detention and writing, 'History repeats itself' a thousand times might make you remember that! Come back here after school.'

Topaz gasped. It was *her* note, not Ruby's, and she couldn't let her friend take the blame!

'That's not fair!' said Topaz.

'Who said that?' Mrs Hornblende spun around and glared at the class. 'I heard someone talking.'

'Me!' said Topaz, putting her hand up, ready to tell the teacher the note wasn't Ruby's. But before she had a chance to admit to launching the paper plane, Mrs Hornblende was looming over her, her short spiky hair pointing like daggers towards Topaz.

'And who are you?' the teacher demanded.

'Topaz,' squeaked Topaz. 'Topaz L'Amour.'

Rosemary Hornblende's eyes glittered. Some of the other teachers had warned her about this pupil. They said she was talented, but a troublemaker.

'Detention and a thousand lines for you too!'

'But—' Topaz began desperately.

'Any more talking and that will be two thousand lines! Now, let's continue our lesson about slavery.'

'I'm so sorry, Rubes,' said Topaz as she walked with Ruby and Sapphire down Constellation Way, looking for Zelma Flint's office. 'I did try to tell Horrid Hornblende it was me, but she wouldn't listen.'

'I know,' said Ruby. 'At least she let us go after half an hour. My hands were aching so much from writing lines, I was worried I'd never be able to play the piano again.'

'And thanks for waiting, Sapphy,' said Topaz. 'Look! I think we're here.'

The three friends stood outside a crumbling large grey building with *Meteor Mansions* hand-painted on to the brickwork.

'Are you *sure* this is it?' Ruby sounded doubtful.

Topaz looked at Zelma Flint's business card: Top Office, 19 Meteor Mansions, Constellation Way, Starbridge.

They were outside the right address, but the building seemed far too shabby to be the offices of a top show business agent.

'Perhaps it's better inside,' she said, pressing a button which said, *Star Management Inc.*

No one answered the intercom, and the girls stood on the pavement, looking up at the windows, not sure what to do next.

'There's no one there,' said Ruby. 'Let's try another time.'

Topaz shook her head. 'What sort of a show business agent closes their offices at five o'clock on a weekday afternoon?' She held her finger on the buzzer. 'There *has* to be someone there.'

From behind the door came the sound of footsteps clattering down the stairs and a high-pitched voice shouted out, 'OK! OK, I'm coming! I'm coming!'

'See!' said Topaz, as the peeling painted door was opened by a thin man wearing a bright pink shirt and *very* tight jeans.

'Jack?' Topaz asked, Jack being the only other person she knew in Zelma's office.

Jack smiled, took two steps back behind the door and then said suspiciously, 'Who are you and why do you want me?'

Topaz stepped into the musty hallway.

'I'm Topaz L'Amour. It's Zelma I've come to see.'

Jack moved forward as if to try to push Topaz back out into the street, but Ruby and Sapphire had already followed her into the building and were blocking the doorway.

'Zelma's out,' he said defensively. 'She won't be back for, oh, days.'

From the top of the building there was a cough and a voice rasped, 'Jack? If you're still down there, pop out and get me a packet of ciggies, will you? I'm gasping for another puff.'

Topaz, Sapphire and Ruby looked up, and hanging over the banisters at the top of the building was the yellow face of Zelma Flint.

'Good heavens!' said Jack, feigning surprise. 'She must have slipped past us when we weren't looking.'

Topaz ignored him and began to climb the stairs to

the top office, past piles of unopened post and free newspapers, parcels which had been delivered but never claimed, and discarded Speedy Snax paper cups and burger wrappers. Off every landing ran a long thin corridor, the door to every office shut, not a soul in sight. This was *not* the type of building Topaz had imagined Zelma Flint inhabited. As a famous show business agent with an office on the top floor, she had always thought of Zelma in a penthouse with floor-to-ceiling windows and views across Starbridge. Shiny, glossy girls would dart about with piles of film scripts, or sit behind sleek desks with top-of-the range computers, chatting on the telephone to film stars and gossiping with theatre directors. There would be a plush reception area with thick carpet, cream sofas and huge vases of expensive lilies sitting on glass-topped tables groaning with the latest copies of all the glossy magazines.

Zelma's office didn't have a cream sofa, or at least, if it did, it was covered with piles and piles of junk. Every surface was littered with towering piles of paper. It was more of a small attic office than a penthouse suite, and if there were views across Starbridge, they couldn't be seen through the filthy windows. Instead of the scent of lilies, there was the putrid stench of stale cigarette smoke. Dotted around the yellow-stained walls of the shabby room were photographs of Zelma pictured with many famous film and television stars.

Sitting behind her desk with her bleached hair, yellow skin and yellow teeth, Zelma almost blended into the background.

On top of a pile of papers on Zelma's desk was a photograph of a girl with blonde curls and a bright white smile. It was in a brown cardboard frame with *Studio Portraits by Lenny 'The Lens'* stamped across the bottom in gold. Topaz took a closer look, and her stomach lurched as she realized the girl in the frame was Octavia Quaver from Rhapsody's Theatre Academy. It was typical of Octavia to have her photograph taken by a professional photographer instead of cramming into a photo booth as Topaz had done. But what was Zelma doing with Octavia's picture?

Zelma continued to rifle agitatedly through the papers on her desk. Without looking up she called out sharply, 'Jack, did you get a new packet?'

Over the girls' heads flew a packet of cigarettes which landed directly in front of Zelma. In one smooth movement, she pulled off the cellophane, flipped open the lid, pulled a white stick from the box, lit it, took a deep breath, coughed, sat back in her chair, gave an oily yellow smile and through a puff of smoke said, 'Ah, Topaz, what can I do for you?'

Topaz took a step forward and said in what she hoped was a confident, firm voice, 'I haven't had payment for *Murder Mile* and I need the money.'

Zelma pretended to look shocked.

'Jack! Can you pull Topaz's file? It appears we owe her some money!'

Jack disappeared into a side office and sounded very busy opening and closing doors and drawers.

At last! thought Topaz. *I'm going to get paid! I can buy a new blazer, treat Mum to something special and there might even be some money left over.*

Zelma's head suddenly jerked to one side as she noticed Sapphire standing in the doorway. She jumped to her feet and, kicking over a pile of paper, rushed round her desk to hold out a nicotine-stained hand.

'Sapphire Stratton!' she gushed. 'How wonderful to meet you. I know your mother, Vanessa, of course. What brings you here?'

'Hello, Miss Flint,' said Sapphire. 'I'm here with Topaz. You owe her money.'

Zelma nodded. 'Jack!' she yelled. 'How are you getting on in there?'

The sound of filing cabinets opening and closing became more frantic.

'I've got just the thing for you!' Zelma tottered back to her desk and, after a brief rummage, waved a piece of paper in the air. 'I shouldn't really be telling you this as it's months away,' she rasped, 'but the Slurp 'n' Burp drinks people are launching a new flavour, Raspberry

Rumble. They're ditching the radio ads and going TV. Big marketing spend, wall-to-wall advertising, the works. Leo Bluff from Bluff, Hype and Bluster tells me they're looking for someone to be the face of Raspberry Rumble. I think you're it!'

Sapphire gave Zelma a polite smile. 'I don't think it's for me, Miss Flint,' she said. 'Thank you anyway.'

'But think!' persisted Zelma. 'You'd be perfect. Sunlit blonde hair, a pretty smile, and a famous family. You wouldn't have to burp of course, we'd get a professional burper in for the voice-over.'

Topaz wondered if Octavia Quaver would be the professional burper. She'd done the radio adverts for Slurp 'n' Burp.

'No, honestly,' said Sapphire firmly.

Zelma shrugged and threw down the piece of paper. She thrust a business card towards Sapphire. 'Think about it. Let me know.'

Jack was still banging filing cabinets in the other room and Topaz began to wonder if he actually *was*

STAR MANAGEMENT INC.

Zelma Flint
THE BEST AGENT IN THE BUSINESS
"I can make you a star"

Top Office
19 Meteor Mansions, Constellation Way
Starbridge, Tel: Starbridge 103

looking for her file, or just standing there, opening and closing drawers.

'And who's this?' Zelma's beady eye fixed on Ruby.

'This is my friend Ruby Ruddle,' said Topaz. 'We're all at Precious Gems.'

'Interesting,' Zelma said, staring at Ruby and taking a long, deep draw on her cigarette. She blew a cloud of smoke into the air. 'Very interesting.'

Ruby blushed crimson and began to chew on the end of one of her plaits.

It seemed to Topaz that *everyone* was interesting to Zelma Flint, except her.

'Prism TV are looking at commissioning a series about a family of computer geeks who find themselves shipwrecked on an island with only a suitcase full of silicon chips. They're thinking of calling it *The Geek Family Robinson*. You'd be perfect as the geeky nerdy daughter.'

'I'm a musician!' said Ruby indignantly, more upset that she had been mistaken for an actress than that Zelma had cast her as a natural nerd.

'Think about it,' Zelma wheezed. 'They're not casting until next year. Let me know.' She tried to push a business card into Ruby's hand, and when she didn't take it, slipped it into the pocket of Ruby's blazer.

Topaz coughed to get Zelma's attention. 'What about me?'

'Jack!' Zelma screeched, and on cue, Jack came scurrying back into the office holding a brown file.

Topaz noticed it didn't have a name on it. It could have been *anyone's* file.

Zelma opened it.

'Aha. Mmm. I see. Yes,' she muttered as behind her, Jack made a great fuss of pointing things out.

Zelma snapped the file shut.

'It seems that the contract you agreed states that the second payment of the fee isn't until the programme is actually transmitted, and that isn't until Christmas.'

'But I haven't had the first payment!' cried Topaz. 'And I didn't sign any contract!'

'Overheads,' said Zelma, tapping the file. 'You *have* been paid, but by the time we've taken our commission fee, the fee for drawing up the contract and the cost of the chaperone to take you to the film set, there's nothing left of the first payment.'

Topaz was shocked. 'But there must be!' she gasped. 'I played two parts. I should have been paid twice!'

Zelma nodded. 'Of course! But two parts meant double the contract fees, double the commission, an additional fee for the double paperwork . . .'

'That's terrible,' said Sapphire. 'In other words, Topaz gets nothing.'

'We only charged for one chaperone, not two,' said Zelma defensively. 'What sort of an agency do you think we are?'

'But I only *had* one chaperone!' said Topaz,

remembering the woman with the rusty red car and snotty-nosed children who had picked her up on the day of filming *Murder Mile*. 'And I think you're a rotten agency.'

'You'll get the rest of the money when the programme airs.'

Zelma got up from her desk and began to walk towards them. With every step forwards, the girls took a step backwards until finally, they were at the door.

Topaz looked Zelma straight in the eye. 'I didn't sign a contract,' she said. 'You *know* I didn't.'

Zelma smiled, showing her yellow peg-like teeth. 'But you did the work!' she crowed. 'You didn't ask to see a contract. By doing the job, with or without a contract, you've agreed to my terms. It's too late to renegotiate now.'

Zelma looked over Topaz's shoulder. 'Ruby, you'd make a perfect geek. Think about it. Sapphire, you could be the face of a fizzy drink. Let me know!'

And with that, Zelma Flint slammed the door in Topaz's face.

Chapter Four

The three friends stood huddled on the landing outside Zelma's office.

'You should report her to Miss Diamond,' said Ruby. '*She'd* get your money for you *and* make sure Zelma doesn't do it again.'

'I can't,' said Topaz miserably.

'But the woman has double-crossed you!' said Sapphire. 'You can't let her get away with it!'

'Double-double-crossed me,' said Topaz bitterly. 'She's done it before. I never got paid for the Speedy Snax voice-over and I couldn't tell Miss D because I didn't tell her I was doing the ad in the first place.'

'But you can tell her about *Murder Mile*, can't you?' said Ruby. 'You did tell her about that, surely?'

Topaz pulled a face and Ruby and Sapphire groaned.

'I thought *this* term you had to keep out of trouble,' said Ruby.

'But *Murder Mile* was *last* term,' said Topaz.

'But it'll be shown *this* term,' said Sapphire. '*Then* what are you going to do?'

'Come on, let's go.' Ruby began to go down the stairs. 'We'll find a café and drown your sorrows in hot chocolate.'

Topaz nodded and trudged after her friends and out into the street. She didn't just feel annoyed that Zelma Flint had refused to pay. She felt hurt that Zelma had offered Ruby and Sapphire parts but ignored her, and was worried about Zelma having Octavia's photograph. Happy Al had warned Topaz to steer clear of Zelma. When he'd been a famous TV star Zelma had been his agent, but the moment his show was cancelled, she stopped returning his phone calls and ignored him. Al had *nothing* good to say about her. Why hadn't she listened to him?

'How about this one?' Sapphire was standing outside a café.

'It's a bit rough,' said Ruby. 'Topaz, what do you think?'

Topaz didn't even look at the café, but pushed open the door and walked in. The moment the door closed behind them, she knew that they'd made a huge

44

mistake. She'd been so busy plotting her revenge on
Zelma Flint, she hadn't even noticed the outside of the
café. Now, standing inside, she looked in horror at the
sea of grey blazers dotted around the tables. They had
stumbled into Grease Galore, the café that the girls
from Starbridge High went to after school. Once, when
she'd been at Starbridge Middle, she'd gone in with
Janice Stone for a dare, but the older girls had made it
quite clear they didn't want juniors in their café and
had chased them out, pelting them with cold chips and
squirting them with tomato sauce. But if there was one
thing Starbridge High girls hated more than junior
pupils in their café, it was girls from other schools. Girls
who dared to go into the café risked having biscuit
crumbs rubbed in their hair and salt poured into their
hot chocolate.

'Let's go somewhere else,' whispered Topaz, too late.

A hush came over the café as hard eyes
glowered at Topaz, Ruby and Sapphire,
who, in their claret blazers with the
Precious Gems logo, were like red
rags to a herd of angry grey bulls.

Sapphire ignored them
and made her way to a
table.

'Let's sit here!' she said.
As she went to sit down, a

girl at a neighbouring table tried to pull the chair out from behind her. But Sapphire was ready for her and was already firmly clutching the edge of the seat.

'Nice try!' she said.

The girls at the table glared back.

Topaz was impressed by how Sapphire had stood up to the girl, but still nervous.

'I *really* don't think this is a good idea,' whispered Ruby through gritted teeth as she sat down. 'Some of these girls look real tough nuts.'

Even the waitress who came over and took their order for three hot chocolates looked nervous. When she came back with the mugs, her hands shook as she put them down.

Topaz was just about to pick up her mug when a grey shadow filled the table.

'Well, if it isn't the stuck-up lot from stage school!'

Topaz looked up and gulped. Kylie Slate was glaring down at her.

'Hello, Kylie,' she said in a voice that came out rather squeakier than she would have liked.

'Look, everyone!' Kylie sneered. 'It's little Miss Wannabe Famous, here with her posh friends in *our* café.'

The girls in grey blazers twittered with sarcastic laughter. Kylie's face turned even harder. She leant towards Topaz and said menacingly, 'Notice I said *our* café. So get out.'

Ruby began to get up but Topaz pushed her back into her seat. *I'm not going to let them intimidate me*, she thought.

'No!' she said defiantly. 'We've paid for these drinks and we're going to stay until we've finished them.'

There was a gasp from the Starbridge High girls.

Kylie looked furious. Her face darkened as she stared nose to nose with Topaz. 'Then we must make you welcome,' she snapped. 'Would you like *sugar* in your hot chocolate?' Kylie grabbed the salt pot, but Topaz, realizing what was about to happen, pulled her mug away so quickly, frothy chocolate milk slopped over the edge and splashed Kylie in the face.

'You!'

To chants of '*Fight! Fight! Fight!*' Kylie lunged towards Topaz, grabbing her hair.

'Leave her alone, Kylie!' a voice shouted out over the chaos.

Janice Stone rushed forward, grabbed Kylie by the back of her blazer and dragged her off Topaz. There was a ripping sound as Kylie staggered backwards holding the right sleeve of Topaz's blazer. Janice grabbed the sorry-looking sleeve from a furious Kylie and handed it back to a shocked and shaken Topaz.

'What did you do that for?' Kylie snarled at Janice, who suddenly didn't look quite so brave.

Janice's voice trembled as she announced to the café, 'Topaz is going to be a star. You've already been in things, haven't you, Topaz?'

Topaz stood in her one-armed torn blazer, holding her ripped sleeve. She just wanted to go home.

'What have you been in?' demanded one of the girls.

'Just stuff,' said Topaz. 'Adverts and things.'

'And you're on TV at Christmas, aren't you?' prompted Janice. 'In some murder mystery thing.'

Topaz nodded.

A murmur of approval rippled round the café.

'Perhaps instead of beating you up I should ask for your autograph!' sneered Kylie sarcastically.

'That's a good idea!' said one of the girls. 'Then if you become famous we can sell it on the internet for *loads* of money.'

There was a sudden scraping of chairs as the girls in grey blazers who just a moment ago had been cheering as Kylie had gone for Topaz, stampeded towards her asking her to sign paper napkins, school books and the backs of bus passes. Topaz was glad that she had spent so many hours practising her large looping autograph.

Finally, the crowd of Starbridge High girls left the café, clutching bits of paper which they hoped would one day be worth something. Topaz looked around for Janice but she had already gone. There was no sign of Kylie either. Sapphire was still sitting at the table looking calm, but Ruby was pale underneath her freckles and was chewing the end of one of her plaits, an untouched mug of stone-cold hot chocolate in front of her.

'Well, that doesn't happen in Happy Al's!' said Topaz, who had enjoyed signing her autograph and being the centre of attention, once Kylie had been dealt with by Janice.

'Thank goodness!' said Ruby. 'Can we go?'

Sapphire took her mobile phone out of her bag and flipped open the cover. 'I'll ring Parks and get him to pick us up from here.' She looked at Ruby. 'He can run you back to the East Wing. Topaz, do you want a lift home?'

Topaz shook her head at the offer of a lift with the Stratton family chauffeur. 'No thanks. I'll jump on a bus. It'll be just as quick. See you tomorrow!'

Stuffing the ripped blazer sleeve into her bag, Topaz gave her friends a hug and stepped out of the café and into the street. It was becoming dark, but the streetlights and car headlamps cast a bright glow as she headed towards the bus stop. In front of her, a dark figure stepped out from a shadowy doorway, blocking the pavement. It was Kylie Slate.

'I'm watching you, little Miss Wannabe Famous,' she said menacingly. 'One day we'll meet when you're not with your posh friends.'

And with that, she melted into the shadows.

Chapter Five

'It's about time you earned your keep, you 'orrible little boy!'

There was silence.

Topaz looked at Miss Diamond, who was sitting at the edge of the room, a script resting on her knee. The Headmistress nodded.

'I said, it's about time you earned your keep, you 'orrible little boy!' Topaz repeated.

Still there was silence.

Miss Diamond rapped her script irritably. 'Jasper! That's twice you've missed your cue. Start concentrating!' She looked across at Topaz. 'Start again and give Jasper his cue. Now, for the third time and without any further prompting . . .'

Topaz stifled a smile. She didn't like Jasper Pretty at the best of times, and *detested* him recently. As the right sleeve of her blazer had been sewn back on for a second time, it was now considerably shorter than the left one, prompting Jasper to spread a rumour that one of Topaz's arms had grown longer than the other, *overnight*!

'It's about time you earned your keep, you *'orrible little boy*!' Topaz curled her tongue around the words, and, for added effect, wagged a finger at him.

Jasper continued to stare dreamily into space and the class began to giggle with embarrassment.

The beads around Adelaide Diamond's neck began to quiver and clack. She rose up from her chair, threw down the script, marched into the centre of the room and glared at Jasper.

'Jasper Pretty, what *is* wrong with you?' she said irritably. 'You are supposed to be reading the part of a young street urchin whose family are about to send him up a chimney to earn money. You're sitting there looking like a cat that got the cream! Start concentrating on this lesson!'

Jasper snapped out of his daydreaming. 'I'm sorry,' he sighed. 'I'm thinking of sparkles and snowflakes rather than soot. I've just heard some *wonderful* news.'

The class leant towards Jasper.

'Which is?' asked Topaz, trying to appear faintly bored, but secretly interested in his news.

'Boris Petrova is bringing his Ice Spectacular to Starbridge!'

There were gasps and cries of 'What?', 'No!', 'When?'

'It's not in Starbridge, it's in Sutton Perry,' corrected Topaz. 'I know because *I'm* going.'

Jasper was beside himself with excitement. 'It *was* supposed to be held at the Sutton Perry Ice Dome, but the roof fell in so it's relocating to Starbridge for one night. They're holding an open audition during half-term for skaters for the Grand Finale, the Dance of One Hundred Snowflakes!'

The classroom filled with the sound of excited chatter.

'That's only two weeks away!'

'I can't wait!'

'Miss Diamond, can we audition?'

'I'll discuss it with you individually,' said the Headmistress. 'Now can we get on?'

The class were far too excited to settle down to the play reading.

'Imagine!' squealed Jasper. 'Silver Lurex, white Lycra and ice-skating all combined. Heaven on ice! I've always longed to play the Ice Prince.' He looked wistful.

'Dream on!' muttered Topaz, just loud enough for Jasper to hear.

'You're just jealous because even if you managed to get a part in the show, you'd only be a lowly snowflake,' Jasper sneered. '*You'd* never be the Ice Princess.'

Miss Diamond clapped her hands and looked irritated. 'Come on, stop dreaming of doing a triple toe-loop in Lycra and concentrate on the play.'

With the class over, Miss Diamond moved around the room, collecting discarded scripts. Topaz approached her and gave a little cough.

'Miss Diamond, I know you said I couldn't take any professional parts this term, but does the ice show count?'

'Of course it does,' the Headmistress said. 'I thought you understood the school won't allow you to take part in *any* performances this term. You have to concentrate on your schoolwork.'

'But Jasper said the auditions are during half-term and the performance is just for one night,' pleaded Topaz. 'It wouldn't interfere with schoolwork, I promise!'

'Are you thinking of auditioning, Sapphire?' asked Miss Diamond.

Sapphire nodded. 'If that's OK, Miss Diamond. I like skating so it might be fun.'

'There you are!' Ruby burst into the room, and then,

seeing Miss Diamond, tried to back out of the door.

The Headmistress beckoned her in.

'Ruby, can you skate?' she asked.

Ruby nodded enthusiastically. 'I've been skating since I was little.'

'Excellent! Then you should audition for the Ice Spectacular too. It will be good practice for your stage fright.'

Ruby turned pale beneath her freckles.

The Headmistress headed towards the door with the pile of scripts clutched to her ample chest. Topaz felt bitterly disappointed. Everyone in her class would be auditioning, even Ruby who didn't want to go!

I bet Octavia is there, thought Topaz, letting out a long, loud sigh. *It's just not fair!*

Miss Diamond paused in the doorway and glanced back to see Topaz's crestfallen face. She knew how much Topaz loved to perform. When she had told her she couldn't do any professional performances she had been thinking of adverts, plays or musicals. What harm could one night in an ice show do?

'This is to be your *only* performance this term and it must *not* interfere with your schoolwork. Do you understand?' she said, before her beads and her heels clickity-clacked down the corridor.

'Yes!' cried Topaz, punching the air with excitement as they followed the Headmistress out. 'I *can* go to the auditions!'

'When Dad suggested we went to the show I didn't expect to have to perform in it,' grumbled Ruby. 'That's not what I call a treat!'

'I hadn't realized you were so keen on skating,' said Sapphire. 'You've never mentioned it before.'

'I'm not,' said Topaz, skipping down the corridor. 'I can't skate.'

Ruby and Sapphire stopped and stared open-mouthed at their friend.

'But you've just convinced Miss D to let you go to the audition!' gasped Ruby.

'Not just any old audition,' corrected Sapphire. 'An audition for the Ice Spectacular. One of the world's most glittering ice shows.'

Topaz shrugged. 'I know. That's why I want to be in it. It's a fabulous chance to perform.' She carried on skipping down the corridor.

'But you can't skate!' called out Ruby, catching up with her. 'Or did you forget you couldn't?'

'Of course not,' laughed Topaz. 'I'm going to have to learn how to skate. I'll start today. Straight after school.'

'The auditions are in two weeks!' said Sapphire. 'Who on earth is going to be able teach you how to skate to professional standard in two weeks!'

Topaz gave her friends her most dazzling smile. 'I was hoping *you* would.'

Chapter Six

'Don't leave me!' Topaz called out desperately, as Sapphire slid out on to the rink and across the ice.

'Just get used to your skates and then stand on the ice until you feel comfortable. I'll be back,' said Ruby as she headed out to join Sapphire.

Topaz stood up on the rubber matting and, stumbling towards the rink, gingerly made her way on to the ice, still clinging like a limpet to the barrier.

'Whoa!' she yelled as she felt her feet give way beneath her, wrenching her arms almost out of their sockets as she continued to grip the barrier. As she pulled herself upright, a small child shot past, sending a spray of ice into her face.

If that tiny tot can skate, so can I, Topaz thought, as

again she tried to put one foot in front of the other, only to stagger and crash into the wall.

Ruby and Sapphire skated up.

'How are you doing?' Sapphire asked.

'I can't even stand on the ice!' Topaz wailed. 'I just keep falling down!'

The girls pointed at Topaz's skates and roared with laughter.

'You've left your skate guards on!' giggled Ruby. 'No wonder you couldn't even stand.'

How was I supposed to know? thought Topaz as she tottered back on to the rubber matting and removed the guards, before wobbling back on to the rink.

She clung to the edge of the barrier. Her knees shook, her ankles ached and already the hired skates were cutting into her heels. Removing the guards had made a *bit* of difference, but not much. She'd barely managed to stagger on to the ice, and now that she was on it, she didn't know what to do next. Everyone else seemed to be confidently gliding round the rink or racing round like little speed demons. Jasper Pretty was obviously taking the audition *very* seriously and was in one corner, doing all the moves they practised in ballet class, but this time, on ice. Sapphire was slowly doing figure-of-eights, her long blonde hair streaming out behind her. But the biggest surprise was Ruby, who gracefully swept across the ice, occasionally doing a little spin or small jump.

'Hello!'

The voice made Topaz jump and she held grimly on to the barrier. It was the pushy first-year, Amber Morelli.

'I hope you're not thinking of auditioning for the Ice Spectacular,' said Topaz. 'Not without the school's permission.'

Amber's eyes lit up. 'I didn't know they were auditioning,' she said unconvincingly. 'But now that I do, I might ask Miss Diamond whether I can audition anyway. I've been skating almost since the day I was born.'

Topaz gave Amber a hard stare and said sharply, 'Miss Diamond won't let you. You're just a first-year.'

Amber flicked her long dark hair. 'I'll *get* permission. If you got permission as a first-year it can't be *that* hard to convince the old trout.'

Topaz was shocked at the way Amber described Miss Diamond. She was *just* like the dreadful Octavia Quaver. Rhapsody's would definitely be a more suitable school for her than Precious Gems.

'If you don't mind, I've an audition to practise for,' said Topaz dismissively, just as a skater shot past at top speed, causing her to wobble alarmingly.

'Are you sure you can skate?' Amber asked suspiciously.

Topaz snorted. 'Like I'd audition for the Ice Spectacular if I couldn't.'

Amber seemed to be expecting her to skate away, so Topaz stood as upright as she dared and pushed off from the side. But barely had she moved, when her legs spun in all directions and she crumpled on to the ice. She tried to get up, but every time she did so, by the time she straightened up, her legs buckled, and down she went again. Eventually, even though she could see Amber watching her, Topaz stayed sitting on the ice, exhausted, her jeans heavy and soaked with water, her gloves dripping wet and her legs too tired to stand. When Jasper had announced they were auditioning for the Ice Spectacular she'd imagined herself like the girl in the bus-stop poster, in a little skating skirt, the blades on her dazzling white boots flashing across the rink whilst adoring fans threw bouquets of flowers tumbling on to the ice. The reality was, instead of white skates she had grey battered hired skates which smelt of egg sandwiches, instead of a skating skirt she had sodden jeans, and the only thing tumbling on the ice was her.

Ruby and Sapphire sped over.

'Are you OK?' they asked, pulling Topaz to her feet.

'Not really,' she muttered, glancing over to see whether Amber was still watching. 'My legs seem out of control.'

'It takes time to get used to the ice,' said Sapphire. Topaz was clinging to her so tightly, her nails dug into Sapphire's arm.

'But I haven't got time!' wailed Topaz. 'I've only got two weeks!'

'Come with us,' said Ruby, holding one of Topaz's hands, whilst Sapphire held the other. 'Now, remember, knees bent, head up, eyes forward.'

Slowly they led their friend around the rink. As long as Topaz kept both her feet on the ice she was fine, but the moment she raised a leg to actually skate, she wobbled so much that Sapphire and Ruby had to use all their strength to keep her upright. At one point, they thought Topaz seemed more confident and tried to let go, but she grabbed their hands so hard, all three of them nearly crashed on to the ice.

'It's no good,' said Topaz despondently, as they headed back towards the edge of the rink. 'I'm just not a natural skater. There's *no way* I'm going to be good enough to even audition, let alone be in the show. I'd just make a fool of myself.'

Ruby and Sapphire gave their friend a sympathetic

look. They knew how much she wanted to audition, how much she loved to perform, but Topaz was right. Even to think about auditioning for the Ice Spectacular was a ridiculous dream.

'You carry on practising,' said Topaz as she clattered off the ice and sank on to a rink-side seat. 'I'll wait for you here.'

Sunlight poured through the skylights on to the gleaming silvery-white ice, and music filled the arena. *Everyone* seemed to be having fun. Even people that began to skate with shaky legs and nervous smiles were soon whooshing around the rink. If they fell down, they just laughed, got up and carried on.

I couldn't even get up! Topaz thought to herself, as she bent down to unlace her skates. She took off the smelly skates, peeled off her socks and examined her sore heels, which sported angry red blisters. They had already burst and were beginning to bleed.

The music stopped.

A siren sounded.

A voice came over the tannoy.

The rink will be closing in five minutes for private lessons. All skaters not here for a private lesson please clear the rink. The private lesson session begins in five minutes!

Skaters started speeding up, skating faster and faster, determined to stay on the ice until the last possible moment. Even Ruby and Sapphire seemed to be involved in a race with a group of boys. Jasper Pretty was still concentrating on the moves he hoped would make him Boris Petrova's natural choice for the Ice Prince.

Suddenly, there was a blur of pink, and a spray of ice showered Topaz as a skater shot past at top speed.

Topaz rubbed the ice out of her eyes. The rink was now almost empty apart from a small figure in a pink skating dress and brilliant white skates who was skating towards her at high speed, head down, arms behind her back. As the skater approached Topaz, she took off, spun twice in the air and landed back on the ice.

'Fantastic double Axel, sweetie!' a shrill female voice yelled out, accompanied by frenzied clapping.

Topaz couldn't decide whether it was the ice or the voice that sent shivers down her spine.

She was still trying to place where she had heard the voice before when there was a whooshing noise, more spraying of ice, and the pink figure skidded to a halt. As Topaz rubbed ice out of her eyes, again, she saw that that the fast-skating, ice-spraying, double-axel-jumping pink figure was none other than Octavia Quaver.

A large woman in a shiny pink tracksuit bustled to the edge of the rink. It was Octavia's mother Pauline. Topaz hadn't seen the gruesome twosome since her summer holiday at Whoosh Waterworld.

Topaz crouched down and pretended to fiddle with her skates, hoping they hadn't seen her.

'Topaz? Are you there?'

She could hear Sapphire and Ruby calling out as they made their way towards her. Topaz ignored the old paper cups and sweet wrappers and crawled even further under the seat.

'What *are* you doing?'

Topaz looked up to see Octavia staring down at her, a sneer stretched across her face. Topaz had crouched so low she was almost lying on the floor. She sat up and, brushing the dust off her wet clothes, said, 'I'd lost a skate. I was just looking for it.'

'If you mean that smelly, mouldy grey-looking thing, it's next to you,' sniffed Octavia. 'And your socks.'

'There you are!' Sapphire and Ruby approached. 'We couldn't see you.'

'She was lying amongst the rubbish on the floor,' said Octavia sarcastically. 'Wasn't she, Mum?'

Pauline Quaver completely ignored Topaz as a small woman dressed head to toe in black skated over.

'My private skating coach,' said Octavia smugly. 'She won an Olympic medal for the height of her jumps.'

'You will make sure Octavia gets the part of the Ice Princess, won't you?' Pauline Quaver barked at the coach. 'We're not paying all this money just for her to be an ordinary snowflake.'

The woman in black gave Pauline a thin, cold smile and skated off with Octavia.

Pauline puffed out her chest as she watched her daughter practise a series of complicated turns, twists, jumps and stops. 'She's been skating almost since the day she was born,' she crowed.

How come everyone *seems to have been skating since they were born except me?* thought Topaz.

Chapter Seven

'Why aren't you turning it off?' Lola peered round her daughter's bedroom door as Topaz's alarm clock continued to ring and ring. 'You'll wake the whole building.'

Topaz ignored the alarm as Lola walked over to her bedside table and silenced the clanging bell.

'Are you ill?' her mother asked, slightly concerned that Topaz continued to lie in bed, staring up at the ceiling.

Topaz tried to shake her head but found she couldn't.

'I can't move!' she said through gritted teeth. 'Everything hurts! It must be from the skating yesterday. I've used muscles I didn't know I had. My body has turned to stone!'

Lola grabbed her daughter's hands and to shrieks of 'Ow!' and 'Aah!' pulled her gently up and out of bed.

'I don't think I can go to school,' whined Topaz. 'Can you ring them?'

'If you get moving the stiffness will go,' said Lola briskly. 'Come on or we'll both be late!'

Topaz walked like a zombie into the bathroom.

It took her *ages* to get ready. Every moment was agony. She groaned when she sat down, she groaned when she stood up. She moaned when she reached up into the cabinet for the toothpaste and grimaced when she tried to clean her teeth. Brushing her hair was just *too* painful. She tottered back into her room and sat on the bed to put on her school uniform.

'Mum!' she yelled. 'I need help!'

Lola popped her head round the door to see Topaz sitting on the edge of the bed, waggling her feet.

'Please could you put my shoes on?' said Topaz weakly. 'I don't think I can bear to bend down.'

Lola gave her daughter a stern look, but grabbed a pair of shoes from under the bed, knelt on the floor and began to push them on Topaz's feet. Her daughter let out a bloodcurdling yell.

'Oh for goodness' sake, Topaz,' snapped Lola, worried she was going to be late for the breakfast shift at Happy Al's. 'It's only a bit of post-skating stiffness.

Anyone would think there was something *really* wrong with you.'

'Blisters!' whined Topaz. 'You were forcing my blistered heels into the shoes. I *bet* they've started bleeding again. Anyway, it's *your* fault I'm in this state.'

Lola looked up at her daughter. 'And how do you work that one out?'

'It's not funny,' grumbled Topaz. 'Everyone but me can already skate. I can't believe that you didn't let me have skating lessons when I was younger.'

'You never asked,' said Lola, laughing.

'You should have *made* me skate,' said Topaz, trying hard to look annoyed, but bursting into a fit of giggles. 'I should have been skating since the day I was born.'

Far from the stiffness wearing off as the day progressed, it seemed to get worse and worse. On the way to school, Topaz grimaced as the bus dipped into potholes, bounced over speed humps and braked a little too sharply. Climbing the steps to the school from Stellar Terrace was slow and painful. During the morning's academic lessons, the teachers were surprised to see that Topaz kept her eyes on the board and her full attention towards the front of the class, unaware that the only reason she wasn't looking down at the copy of *Snapped!* magazine hidden between the pages of her exercise book was because she couldn't move her neck.

'How long do you think it will last?' she asked, as Sapphire helped her get ready for Anton Graphite's dance class that afternoon. 'It seems to be getting worse rather than better.'

Sapphire shrugged. 'Are you just stiff, or do you think you've actually damaged something? You did fall down a *lot*.'

Topaz wasn't sure. Just as one bit of her body stopped aching, another bit started.

Ruby put her head round the door. She looked pale and nervous. The sheet music she was holding was quivering.

'Anton has asked me to tell you to bring *all* your dance shoes into the lesson,' she announced to the locker room in a shaky voice. 'Oh, and I'm playing the piano.'

She darted back out.

'What's that all about?' asked Topaz, dragging her dance shoes out of her locker.

'No idea,' said Sapphire. 'But Ruby looked terrified.'

* * *

In the dance studio, pupils were practising pliés, stretching their legs and flexing their feet. Topaz dropped her shoes on to the floor and leant on the barre. In one corner, Ruby was sitting rigidly at the piano, beads of sweat forming across her pale forehead. A year at Precious Gems had done nothing to cure her crippling stage fright, but Miss Diamond and Gloria Gold were determined that she should have as much practice as possible in performing in front of an audience. Playing the piano for the class was a start.

Dance teacher and choreographer, Anton Graphite, bustled into the room.

'Everyone warmed up?' he shouted in a clipped voice. 'Remember, a cold muscle is an injured muscle!'

The class nodded and murmured, 'Yes.'

Topaz said nothing.

The dance choreographer had a smug look on his face and a gleam in his eye.

'You're probably wondering why I asked you to bring *all* your dance shoes. I thought this afternoon we'd do a grading session! An exam across three dance styles!'

A wave of panic swept through the class. They'd had no time to practise or perfect their routines. Topaz was glad she had the barre to hold on to, as the announcement from Anton Graphite made her feel faint.

'Fifteen minutes each of tap, jazz and ballet!' Anton called out as pupils scuttled off to change into their tap-shoes. 'Marks out of ten for each section!'

'Tell him you're injured!' whispered Sapphire as she crouched beside Topaz, helping her into her tap-shoes. 'You can't dance like this.'

Topaz pulled a face. 'I *promised* Miss D that the skating wouldn't interfere with my lessons. Anyway, you know what she and Anton would say, don't you? The show must go on!'

'But not when you're in such a state,' replied Sapphire. 'Topaz, please! Pull out of the class.'

'Hurry up and stop talking!' Anton called out as he stood in the centre of the room.

The class watched as Anton showed them a routine whilst they mimicked him, tracing the steps on the floor.

'I'll do it once more with you to music, then you repeat it until I tell you to stop! Ruby? We're ready!'

Ruby began to play the piano, as Anton Graphite and the class tippity-tapped their way around the room, across the room and up and down the room. Topaz's legs felt like planks of wood and her ankles like solid stone. She could feel the blisters on the back of her heels beginning to rub raw again, blood oozing through her tights. Her neck was so stiff she could hardly turn it, and her movements seemed to be always slightly behind everyone else's.

'Really feel the rhythm!' Anton yelled out over the clatter of tapping feet. 'Feel every step!'

I'm feeling every step all right! thought Topaz. As the metal taps on her shoes struck the floor, her entire body seemed to quiver with pain.

She noticed the teacher sitting at the side of the studio, scribbling frantically in a pink notebook. Every so often, he would glance in Topaz's direction, frown and scribble again.

After a while, Anton told them to stop and ordered everyone to change into trainers for jazz. After the stiff-soled tap-shoes, the air-cushioned trainers felt wonderful, but Topaz's comfort was short-lived as Ruby upped the tempo of the piano music, whilst Anton Graphite demonstrated a routine filled with hip thrusts and pike jumps.

'Use your entire body!' shouted Anton as the class swayed to the rhythm. 'Use your arms, your legs, your everything!'

I'm trying! Topaz thought desperately, as she attempted to raise her arms above her head without grimacing. Even Ruby shot her a despairing look as Topaz danced by the piano, stiff as a robot.

'How are you doing?' whispered Sapphire, as they changed into their ballet-shoes for the final section.

'Badly,' replied Topaz. 'I'm in agony.'

Ballet was one of Topaz's favourite classes. Before

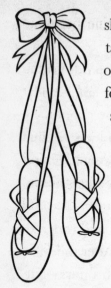

she'd come to Precious Gems she'd never taken a proper ballet class, whereas some of her fellow pupils had been doing ballet for years. But extra practice and after-school classes with the PTs had paid off, and she was every bit as good as the others in her class. Topaz was desperate to start pointe work, and even though Anton Graphite had told them horror stories of pupils who had been too impatient to wait and had ended up with *terrible* feet, she'd stuff the end of her soft ballet-shoes with tissues and stagger about her bedroom, pretending to be on the tips of her toes. Sometimes, she'd find one of the blocked shoes an older pupil had left lying around and would lovingly feel the solid end encased in pink satin, dreaming of the day when she would have her own pair. But today, she might as well have been dancing in lead-lined wellington boots.

There was worse to come. The routine that Anton had asked them to perform ended with a left side split. At first, Topaz had never managed to get her legs to stretch out either side of her, but months of gentle exercise and practice now meant the splits was one of her best moves. However badly she had done in the exam so far, this was her final chance to impress Anton Graphite.

I must do this! she thought as the routine began to reach its conclusion. *I can do this!*

As Ruby played the final bars of music, with gritted teeth and eyes watering with pain, Topaz slid her feet along the dance floor and her legs followed until she was lying gracefully on the floor, her left leg stretched out in front and her right leg beautifully straight behind her. She'd done it! Despite the pain and the stiffness, she had finished the routine with one graceful movement.

'Well done, everyone,' said Anton, clapping. 'I'll let you know the results.'

The class began to leave the dance studio, chatting about the routines, despairing at missed movements or poor performances. Ruby, despite being nervous at the start of the lesson, had enjoyed playing the piano and was still running her hands up and down the keys.

Anton Graphite looked up from scribbling some last-minute observations in his notebook.

'Topaz!' he snapped. 'The class is finished, or didn't you notice?'

'I know,' squeaked Topaz.

'Then why are you still doing the splits?' Anton demanded, staring down at her.

Topaz looked up at the dance teacher and said weakly, 'I'm afraid I'm stuck. I can't get up!'

Topaz stood in the corridor outside Miss Diamond's study. At the end of assembly the morning after the afternoon of the disastrous dance exam, Miss Diamond had asked to see her. Her voice had made it quite clear that Topaz was in trouble.

The door of the study was open and the pink light bulbs studded around the edge of a large mirror cast a soft rosy glow, but there was no sign of the Headmistress. Topaz could see Miss Diamond's five Golden Nugget Awards standing in a line at the front of a large glass cabinet filled with trophies and awards. Next to the Golden Nuggets stood the gold plastic whisk Ruby and Topaz had won in their first term at Precious Gems, on the TV game show *Proof of the Pudding*. Lining the walls were photographs, posters and newspaper articles, all showing a radiant young Adelaide Diamond at the height of her film and stage career.

The sound of footsteps approached as Miss Diamond appeared, together with a stony-faced Anton Graphite. Topaz's stomach lurched as she followed them into the study.

'Sit down, Topaz,' said the Headmistress in a clipped, icy voice.

Topaz looked at the leather armchairs and hesitated. Last time she sat on them they'd burped like a whoopee cushion. She lowered herself gently on to the smooth leather and was relieved to hear only a small squeak.

Miss Diamond sat at her desk as Anton Graphite hovered nearby, his lips pursed, a look of contempt on his face.

'Your class had an exam yesterday,' said the Headmistress. 'Anton has been to see me about your results.'

Anton nodded and folded his arms across his chest.

'Three points out of thirty!' Miss Diamond said, her eyebrows rising so high they disappeared into her hairline. 'One point for each section!'

Anton Graphite frowned and said witheringly, 'No one has *ever* got such a low score.'

'Was it *all* bad?' Topaz asked. She knew she had done badly, but not *that* badly.

From his back pocket, Anton pulled out the pink notebook.

'Let me see,' he said, flipping through the pages. 'Yes, it was *all* bad.'

'Even ballet?' asked Topaz.

'*Especially* ballet,' sneered the teacher. 'Your pliés

were poor, your arabesques appalling and your pirouettes pathetic.'

'What did I get the three points for?' Topaz asked, and then wished she hadn't.

'Turning up,' Anton snorted. 'Though I don't know why you bothered.'

Adelaide Diamond ran her hands through her wiry grey hair and looked at the second-year who was staring forlornly into her lap. Several times a term, every term, a teacher would storm in and complain about Topaz. Usually it was the academic staff upset that Topaz wasn't working, or had set fire to the classroom, or daydreamed in lessons. But stage classes were different. Whilst far from perfect technically, Topaz had always shown energy, enthusiasm and hard work, so it had been a surprise when Anton Graphite had been to see her about Topaz's appalling exam results.

'This isn't like you, Topaz,' said the Headmistress. 'What went wrong?'

Topaz bit her lip and mumbled into her lap, 'I was injured.'

Anton Graphite's face was a picture. 'Injured!' he exploded. 'What were you thinking of? You could have ruined your career, dancing with an injury.'

Topaz avoided the gaze of both teachers and said, 'But the school is always telling us that the show must go on. So I went on.'

Adelaide Diamond looked exasperated. 'You should have known better than to dance with an injury. Is it a strain or a sprain? Have you seen a doctor?'

Topaz shook her head.

'Then you must! I'll ring your mother to arrange it.'

The Headmistress pulled out a sheet of headed notepaper from a letter rack in front of her and began to write. 'Now, where are you injured?'

Topaz sat in silence.

Miss Diamond looked up. 'Ankle? Left leg? Right leg? Calf? Thigh?'

'Umm . . .' Topaz didn't know what to say.

'You *must* know what part of you is injured!' snapped Anton.

'Sort of all over,' said Topaz sheepishly, adding, 'But I'm fine today.'

'Oh, so miraculously your injuries have healed?' Anton Graphite shot the Headmistress a suspicious look. 'That seems *very* odd!'

Miss Diamond put down her pen, pushed back her chair and said slowly, 'Is there something you're not telling us, Topaz?'

Topaz looked nervously from the Headmistress to the dance teacher and back again before admitting, 'I went skating the day before the exam and was so stiff I could hardly walk, let alone dance.'

'Skating!' Miss Diamond said tersely. 'Skating for the Ice Spectacular auditions?'

Topaz nodded. 'Lots of the others went. Sapphire was there!'

'But she didn't fail the exam!' said Anton. '*You* did!'

'She didn't fall down as much as me!' Topaz replied. 'Sapphire could already skate!'

Anton gasped. Adelaide glared. The atmosphere in the study became icy cold. Miss Diamond rose slowly to her feet. The beads around her chest began to rise and fall alarmingly, clacking together in double-quick time.

'Are you telling me that you asked to attend the auditions, knowing full well you couldn't skate?' Miss Diamond's voice was almost a low growl.

'I was going to learn!' Topaz said. '*Everyone* seemed to be going to the auditions except me!'

'But *they* could already skate!' roared Anton Graphite. 'What were you thinking of, you silly girl?'

'I didn't realize it would be so hard,' admitted Topaz. 'Skaters make it look so easy.'

'But that's what ballet-dancers do and you know how hard ballet is!' Anton Graphite waved his pink notebook in the air with frustration.

'Are you still planning to go to the audition?' Miss Diamond asked.

Topaz's face lit up and she nodded enthusiastically.

'I've got two weeks to learn to skate. I'm sure I'll be better next time. And maybe I could get some private lessons, somehow.'

Adelaide Diamond shook her head. 'When I gave you permission to go to the auditions it was on the understanding that it wouldn't interfere with your schooling. It already has. I'm withdrawing my permission.'

'But you can't!' Topaz gasped. 'Please! Miss Diamond! I have to go!'

She thought of Octavia zooming around the ice rink in her little skating dress. Even if Topaz couldn't be the Ice Princess, at least being a snowflake would still be a chance to perform in front of an audience and under a spotlight.

Miss Diamond was firm.

'No auditions, no appearances, no professional engagements. Nothing. One more problem, Topaz, and your scholarship will be withdrawn.'

Chapter Eight

'Candidates for the open audition for the Ice Spectacular to the left!' shouted a woman holding a clipboard in one hand and a camera in the other. 'Parents, chaperones and supporters to the right!'

Topaz gave Ruby and Sapphire a weak smile and said, 'Good luck.'

Before her friends had a chance to say anything, they were swept along in the crowd of excited skaters, all hoping to be chosen for the Grand Finale of Boris Petrova's Ice Spectacular, the Dance of One Hundred Snowflakes. Topaz really did wish her friends luck, although the thought of watching Octavia, Jasper and so many of her other classmates glide around the rink, whilst she sat on the sidelines, was almost too much to bear. But Ruby and Sapphire were her best friends and she wanted to be there to support them, and besides, there was nothing else to do during half-term.

The weeks at school leading up to the audition had been hard. Everyone seemed excited about the ice show and took every opportunity to talk about it. Topaz felt left out. Every morning on the way to school she looked at the poster at the bus stop and glared at the picture of the girl in a little silver skating dress and bright white boots, clutching a spray of red roses.

That could have been me! she thought. *Now it's going to be Octavia Quaver.*

Topaz made her way to the café at the side of the rink, ordered a hot chocolate and sat down. She could already see people beginning to warm up, stretching their legs and rubbing their muscles, each hopeful skater wearing a number stuck to their back. The boys wore tracksuits and most of the girls wore leotards with skating skirts, but at the far side of the rink, Octavia Quaver was practising her turns in a bright pink skating dress scattered with silver sequins. Jasper Pretty was already flashing around the rink, trying to impress Boris Petrova before the auditions started. In the viewing gallery at the front of the rink, Pauline Quaver

sat next to a glum-looking girl holding a pile of bags and clothes. Topaz recognized her as Octavia's friend Melody Sharp.

A loudspeaker burst into life.

'Welcome to the open auditions for the Ice Spectacular!'

A ripple of excitement spread across the ice, which was now full of skaters eager to impress.

'Please welcome ice impresario and choreographer extraordinaire, Boris Petrova!'

The assembled skaters clapped and cheered as a small man holding a microphone and wearing a tight black all-in-one skating suit glided across the rink into the spotlight.

'Welcome, my friends!' said Boris in a heavy foreign accent. 'It is good to see so many young skaters eager to perform.'

There was more clapping and cheering.

'This will not take long. I know what I want and I know when I see it! Snowflakes later. First, I choose the Ice Prince and Ice Princess!'

A small group of skaters, including Jasper and Octavia, stayed on the rink whilst most of Topaz's classmates, including Sapphire and Ruby, made their way to the edge to wait their turn.

There's even a first-year here! Topaz thought bitterly, as she watched the dark-haired figure of Amber Morelli practising turns on the ice. *She obviously thinks she's princess material!*

Boris showed the group a series of moves, and as the music floated over the loudspeakers, the skaters moved around the ice as if performing a ballet on ice. Some of the skaters were obviously more snowflake than star standard as they tried jumps that were too high or spins that were too fast and landed, heavily, on their bottoms.

Topaz watched Octavia and Jasper float effortlessly around the rink. Jasper had a dreamy look on his face whilst Octavia looked focused and determined. Boris seemed impressed. He stood on the ice, his hands flapping like an overexcited seal.

'Enough!' he shouted out after only a few minutes. 'I've found my ice royalty!'

The music stopped and the rink, packed with anxious parents eager to see their children do well, held its breath.

'The Prince is number eighteen and the Princess number one!'

85

Jasper dropped to his knees with delight and Octavia gave a smug smile. At the edge of the rink Pauline Quaver jumped up and down shouting, 'Yes! Yes! Yes!', knocking Melody Sharp on the head.

The skaters who hadn't been chosen slowly skated to the side of the rink, their heads down, crushed with disappointment. Boris announced there would be a short break before he began to choose the snowflakes.

Topaz waved at Sapphire and Ruby on the other side of the rink, but they seemed deep in conversation with a group of girls Topaz had never met.

If only I could go home – but I promised I'd be here for them, Topaz thought miserably.

Amber Morelli suddenly staggered on to the rubber matting and collapsed on to the seat next to her.

'Topaz!' she gasped. 'Thank goodness! The blade on one of my skates has come loose and now it's bent. I'll have to use a crummy hired pair. Can you go and get me some?'

Topaz gave the first-year a hard stare.

'Please?' added Amber, desperately.

'I thought I told you, Miss Diamond doesn't allow first-years to attend auditions without permission,' said Topaz sourly. 'You'll be in *big* trouble if she finds out.'

'I've got permission,' snapped Amber. 'And Miss Diamond won't be happy if she knows you haven't been helpful to a first-year.'

Topaz didn't know whether to be furious with Amber for being a pushy first-year or with Miss Diamond for giving Amber the chance to audition. But if she didn't help Amber with her broken skate, the horrid girl would *definitely* squeal on her and Topaz could find herself in yet *more* trouble.

'Stay here,' she said, stomping off.

'What size?' asked the girl behind the counter when Topaz finally managed to work her way through the crowds to the skate-hire kiosk.

'I don't know,' said Topaz. 'Sort of my size, I guess, maybe smaller.'

The girl looked down at Topaz's feet and then tossed a pile of skates on the counter. 'See if those are any good.'

Topaz picked up the greying boots, slung them over her shoulder and began to make her way back to the rink. As she got closer, someone suddenly grabbed her arm. It was the clipboard woman from earlier.

'There's always one!' said the woman, grabbing a startled Topaz by the right arm and marching her towards the rink. 'Name?'

'Er . . . Topaz L'Amour,' said Topaz, bewildered. 'But I'm not—'

'Stop!' ordered the woman, as she grabbed the camera dangling round her neck and pointed it at

Topaz who blinked furiously as the flash exploded in her face.

'No! You don't understand, I'm not—'

'Get your skates on and get on to the rink.' The woman peeled a large sticky label with number two hundred on it and slapped Topaz hard on the back. 'You're going to be late for the audition. Good luck!'

Topaz stood at the side of the rink. She *could* have tried harder to tell the clipboard woman that she wasn't here for the audition. She *should* have taken the skates back to Amber Morelli. But here she was about to audition for the part of a snowflake, dressed in jeans, a sweatshirt and a pair of skates which were at least one size too small.

'It wasn't my idea!' said Topaz, as an astonished Ruby and Sapphire skated up. 'I was forced into it!'

'A snowflake is a simple part but an important part,' Boris announced.

Topaz continued to hold on to the side of the rink in a way which she hoped looked casual, even though she felt she was clinging on for dear life.

'I need poise, speed and flair,' said Boris. 'There are no snowflake rehearsals before the show. After the Ice Prince has done his solo, you skate out with the sleigh holding the Ice Princess, and skate in a circle round the sleigh when they meet again.'

Topaz could see Amber Morelli waving at her from across the rink. She looked *furious*.

Boris was still giving out instructions.

'To start, hold hands and skate slowly round. Now go!'

Sapphire grabbed one of Topaz's hands and Ruby grabbed the other, and pulling her towards the other skaters, they formed a chain.

Knees bent, head up, eyes forward. Knees bent, head up, eyes forward. Topaz repeated to herself as the chain went round the rink.

'Faster! Faster!' Boris yelled.

Knees bent, head up, eyes forward, Topaz continued to chant in her head as the line of skaters picked up speed.

Faster and faster the chain skated until Boris told them to drop hands and come to a sudden stop when he gave them the signal. Topaz realized with horror that whilst she had become used to going round the rink and was even beginning to quite enjoy it, she had no idea how to stop. The only way she had stopped before was by falling down.

'Stop!'

Everyone dropped hands and there was the sound of sharp blades turning as ice flew up.

I'm going to fall! thought Topaz, grabbing on to the nearest object to steady herself. Unfortunately, the object nearest to her was one of Ruby's plaits, and in grabbing it, Topaz pulled Ruby backwards on to the ice with a sharp thud, propelling herself forward at top speed.

I can't stop! thought Topaz in horror as she hurtled across the ice on one leg, the other stretched out behind her.

'Speed and style! My first snowflake!' Boris called out as Topaz flashed past him managing a smile and a wave, zoomed through a gap in the barrier, across the rubber matting and landed in the lap of a startled and furious Amber Morelli.

'I'm going to tell the Headmistress you *deliberately* stopped me from auditioning,' snapped Amber, pushing Topaz away.

'Do that,' smiled Topaz, 'and I'll tell her you called her an old trout.'

Chapter Nine

'You've *got* to help me,' pleaded Topaz. 'I've *got* to learn how to skate properly! I don't suppose either of you would teach me?'

'No,' said Sapphire firmly. 'Ruby and I don't want you to leave Precious Gems, and if Miss D finds out, you'll be in big trouble.'

'But I didn't *mean* to be a snowflake,' said Topaz. 'It just happened.'

'But going to the actual show won't *just happen*, will it?' said Ruby, gingerly lowering herself into a chair in Happy Al's. Falling on the ice had meant a nasty ice burn on her bottom and no role as a snowflake. Topaz had said she felt *terrible* that she'd pulled Ruby over, but Ruby was secretly relieved she wouldn't have to perform in the ice show.

'Face it, Topaz,' said Sapphire. 'Even if you learn to skate in time, if Miss D finds out, she'll go potty.'

'You must pull out,' said Ruby. 'You know you have to.'

Topaz fiddled with the salt and pepper pots on the table.

'I suppose so, but I can't bear it!' she groaned. 'This was my only chance of performing all term!'

'Hello!' Happy Al sauntered over to their table. 'What can I get you?'

The girls eyed him suspiciously.

'Two cheese toasties between three, please,' said Topaz.

Al beamed at her. 'Coming right up!'

The girls could hear him whistling to himself as made their cheese toasties.

'That's *really* weird,' said Topaz, watching Al pottering about behind his counter. 'He looks like Al, he talks like Al and he's in Al's café, but he seems so happy he can't be Al. Can he?'

Ruby shrugged. 'He didn't even complain when we asked for two toasties between three of us.'

'*And* he came to our table,' said Sapphire. 'He seemed almost helpful. I've only ever seen him scowling, never smiling.'

'Three cheese toasties!' Al said, bringing them over to their table.

Topaz looked at the money she was about to hand over. 'Um . . . we only ordered two. We don't have the money for three.'

'Have the third on the house!' said Al. 'Free. On me.'

'Are you all right?' Ruby asked him. 'You seem very happy. What's happened?'

Al gave a furtive smile, reached into his back pocket and pulled out a crumpled piece of paper torn from a magazine. It was the 'Screen Snippets' section from *Snapped!* He waved it in the air before tossing it on the table.

'It's here in black and white,' he said triumphantly. '*Murder Mile* is to be shown in a couple of weeks. Look! There's a write-up.'

Topaz grabbed the article.

Here's something to look forward to – Murder Mile *is due to return to our screens for a Christmas special in early December! When a young girl is found dead in a muddy field on Christmas Day, Inspector Barry 'Nosey' Parker is brought in to investigate in a sparkling special episode of this classic TV cop series. The mystery to us is why this series was ever off our screens in the first place!*

Buy your copy of Snapped! *to get the date, channel and time!*

'Oh no,' gasped Topaz, pushing away the article. 'This is a disaster, maybe even another disastrophe!'

'I thought you'd be pleased,' said Al, looking put out. He grabbed the article off the table and stuffed it back in his pocket. 'I wouldn't have shown you if I thought you'd go all huffy.'

He stomped back behind the counter and began to furiously polish the chrome Turbo Frother cappuccino machine with a tea towel.

'*I* thought you'd be pleased,' said Sapphire. 'It's great that it's about to be shown.'

'And then Zelma Flint will have to pay you,' added Ruby.

Topaz sighed and rested her head on the plastic red-and-white checked tablecloth. Only a few weeks ago she would have been thrilled to see *Murder Mile* in the TV listings. She was desperate to appear on television, and couldn't wait to see her name roll up on the end-credits for two parts, Abigail and Alice. Zelma Flint would have to pay her and she could buy another blazer, one with matching arms. The girls from Starbridge High would see her. People all over the country would watch. A famous casting agent might spot her and see that she was perfect for a leading role. There was just one problem. She looked up at her friends.

'When Miss D finds out, I'll be expelled.'

'Expelled!' gasped Ruby. 'I thought you said she would pull your scholarship.'

Topaz looked embarrassed. 'She knows we couldn't afford the fees, so without the scholarship I'd have to leave. It's almost the same as being expelled.'

'Do you *really* think she'd do that?' asked Sapphire.

'I don't know.' Topaz picked long strings of cold cheese from her toastie. 'I was hoping it wouldn't be shown until term had broken up and she'd already given me another scholarship.'

'So tell her now,' said Ruby. 'Come clean now.'

Topaz didn't think that was a good idea.

'I might as well leave being expelled until the last minute.'

'Well, it's done now,' said Sapphire. 'You can't turn the clock back so you might as well celebrate your TV debut. We should do something the night it's on. We could watch it together or—'

Her phone rang.

Sapphire looked at the display and groaned. 'It's Mum's assistant. I wonder what he wants?'

She flipped open the slim silver cover. 'Hi. Rupert.'

Muffled sounds came from the other end.

'What, again?' Sapphire said irritably. 'She's only just come back!'

There was the sound of high-pitched chatter.

'Whatever. Tell her to come here. I'm in Happy Al's Café. Twelve Galaxy Street. Just round the corner from the school. I'll get a taxi home.'

She snapped the phone shut and rolled her eyes.

'Apparently, Mum is *so* exhausted from filming a two-hour television special she says she needs *another* holiday.' There was an icy edge to Sapphire's voice. 'The director Joshua P. Finkleberg has invited her to stay on his private island. She's on her way to the airport now.'

'Are you going to see her?' asked Topaz, remembering how she'd met Sapphire's film-star mother, Vanessa, in the first-class lounge at Starbridge International Airport.

Sapphire shook her head. 'Rupert suggested Parks could pick me up, take Mum to the airport and then run me home, but that could take *hours*. I'm not hanging around an airport lounge again. I've told her to come here.'

Topaz wondered whether Vanessa Stratton would recognize her. Despite having met Topaz several times, Sapphire's mother *never* seemed to remember her.

Sapphire's phone rang again.

'Where are you? What? No way! She can't be *that* tired.'

She ended the phone call and looked annoyed.

Ruby patted her on the arm. 'Everything all right?'

Sapphire angrily spun her phone on the table. 'She's too tired to come and see me. She wants me to go and see her.'

'At the airport?' Topaz asked.

'No, in the car outside,' replied Sapphire. 'She says she's too tired to get out.'

Topaz and Ruby craned their necks towards the window. A huge black limo waited outside, its engine still running.

'Don't let her see you!' gasped Sapphire, pulling Topaz back from the window. 'I don't want her to think we're interested.'

'But I am!' said Topaz.

'She *is* your mum,' said Ruby. 'Don't you think you should go out?'

Sapphire said nothing. The three of them sat in silence, staring into space for what seemed like *ages*. Eventually the door to the café opened, and in floated international film star Vanessa Stratton. She paused in the doorway, the light framing her perfect blonde bob, her diamonds sparkling.

Al, instantly recognizing Sapphire's mother and amazed to see a real-life celebrity in his café, rushed over.

This is definitely the time to put the Turbo Frother cappuccino machine through its paces, he thought to himself. *Wait until she sees the multi-directional froth nozzle and turbo steam jet!*

'Could I get you a cappuccino, Miss Stratton?' he

asked, proudly gesturing towards the gleaming chrome machine.

Without even looking at him, Vanessa wrinkled her nose and said with a mixture of disgust and pity, 'Cappuccinos are *so* last year. I'll have a skinny soya venti latte with an extra shot and a dash of hazelnut syrup, white cap, no dusting.'

'Then it's instant,' Al snapped, stomping back behind the counter.

'Hello, Mum!' Sapphire waved at her mother.

Rupert, who had been hovering in the background, grabbed a chair, polished it with a linen handkerchief and pushed it towards the table.

'Watch the hair and make-up, darling,' said Vanessa, perching on the polished chair and patting her hair as Sapphire leant over to give her a kiss. 'Rupert has told Scoop Mackenzie I'll be at the airport so I want to look decent for the pictures.'

Rupert produced a small mirror. Vanessa glanced into it, smiled at herself and nodded before Rupert whipped it away and melted into the background.

'It was *so* mean of you not to come out to the car, darling. You know how absolutely *exhausted* I get filming. I give my all to even the smallest project. You'll understand one day.'

'I am *not* going to be an actress,' said Sapphire firmly. 'I *keep* telling you.'

Vanessa ignored her and pointed a perfectly manicured finger at Ruby and Topaz. 'Who are these people?'

'Mum!' growled Sapphire. 'Don't you remember? I went on holiday with them in the summer!'

'Of course,' laughed Vanessa. 'Only teasing!'

Topaz gave a sigh of relief. Vanessa *had* remembered her after all.

'Tracey and Rosie. How are you?'

Sapphire groaned. 'It's Topaz and Ruby!'

'Whatever,' said Vanessa dismissively. 'What was so important that you couldn't come out to the car and save my tired but very shapely legs?'

'We were planning how to celebrate Topaz's debut on television,' said Sapphire.

Vanessa Stratton raised an arched eyebrow in Topaz's direction.

'I'm in the Christmas special of *Murder Mile*,' said Topaz. 'So is Al.' She pointed to Al, whose familiar frown was back on his face. 'He played Inspector Barry "Nosey" Parker in the original series and he's back for the special.'

Vanessa let out a long, deep sigh. 'Sapphire, why aren't you in something like that? I've told you, I could get you lots of wonderful roles without you even auditioning.'

Before Sapphire could say anything, Topaz piped

up, 'Sapphire is skating in the Ice Spectacular at the end of term!'

Vanessa Stratton's eyes lit up. Finally her daughter was going to perform! Perhaps a taste of show business would put all this nonsense about being a doctor or a scientist out of her mind.

'That's wonderful news, darling! Why didn't you telephone Rupert so he could let me know? I'll be at the opening night to support you, of course!'

Sapphire looked embarrassed. 'I'm just a snowflake in the Dance of One Hundred Snowflakes. It's only on for one night.'

Vanessa looked taken aback. 'You mean that you are in the chorus line? You are just one of a hundred other snowflakes? You don't have a major part?'

'The snowflakes are very important!' said Topaz, leaping to Sapphire's defence. 'And Sapphire will make a beautiful snowflake.'

Vanessa Stratton was unimpressed. She ignored Sapphire and, turning to Topaz, asked, 'Who's doing the catering for your screening party? I can thoroughly recommend Celestial Canapés. The waiters they provide are divine!'

Topaz looked blank, Ruby looked amused and Sapphire still looked embarrassed.

'Don't tell me you're not having a screening party,' cried Vanessa. '*Everyone* has a screening party!'

Rupert approached their table, tapped his watch and pointed towards the door.

'Time to go!' said Vanessa, getting up from her seat. 'If I'm to have any hope of joining Joshua for cocktails I'd better get to the airport.'

Sapphire bit her lip. *I should be used to this by now*, she thought. *Just a few snatched moments between holidays and film sets. That's all the time Mum gives me.*

Vanessa began to leave but Sapphire continued to sit at the table, staring into space. Rupert hovered nervously at the door. He was hoping Sapphire wouldn't cause a scene. He'd never forgotten her throwing a tantrum at the airport in full view of the show business reporter from *The Starbridge Gazette*.

At the door, Vanessa swung round. 'Sapphire, aren't you at least going to come out and see me off?'

Sapphire sat rigidly at the table, staring into space. Topaz and Ruby knew she was trying hard not to cry.

'Will you be coming to the Ice Spectacular?' she asked.

Vanessa looked uncomfortable. 'Ah, about the ice show. I thought you had a proper part, one which would name you in the programme. I'd just be watching a crowd if I came.'

'So you won't come,' said Sapphire flatly.

Vanessa Stratton could see Sapphire was upset. 'I've an idea,' she said. 'Why don't you throw a screening party for Tracey at the mansion? I'll come back for it! That will be fun, won't it? I can spend time with you and all your little friends. You know how much I love a party.'

Sapphire said nothing. She couldn't even be bothered to remind her mother that she'd got Topaz's name wrong, again.

Vanessa looked across at Topaz. 'Would you like that?'

'Yes please!' gushed Topaz, who had only seen pictures of Sapphire's house in *Celebrity Pools & Patios*. 'That would be *fantastic*. Thank you so much!'

Sapphire glared at her mother. 'Do you *promise* to come back for the party?' she asked. '*Really* promise?'

'Of course,' purred Vanessa Stratton. 'Just ring Rupert and let him know when it is. I'll be there.'

Topaz, Ruby and Sapphire stood on the pavement outside Happy Al's and waved as the long dark limousine pulled out into the traffic and sped away. In the fading light Ruby and Topaz noticed Sapphire brush away a tear.

'She'll be back in a couple of weeks,' said Ruby, putting her arm around her friend. 'She said she'd be back for the party.'

'I'm not crying because she's gone away,' said Sapphire, as more tears rolled down her cheeks. 'I'm crying because I know she's made a promise she can't keep. She won't be at the party. Something will happen. There'll be a better party or a sudden holiday invitation or some last-minute emergency like a broken nail which will be more important than me.'

'But she promised!' said Topaz, who couldn't imagine her own mother ever letting her down. 'She'll be there!'

Sapphire shook her head. 'Something will go wrong. You just wait and see.'

Chapter Ten

'We need to think about your screening party,' said Sapphire, pulling out a pen and a sheet of paper from her bag. 'We haven't got long to plan it and Nanny Bean wants to know how much food she should do.'

Topaz's stomach lurched. The TV guides had announced that the Christmas special of *Murder Mile* was going to be shown on the first Thursday in December, just over a week away. Topaz didn't know whether to be thrilled or terrified. One moment she was excited about the thought of being on television, the next plunged into despair at the prospect of Miss Diamond finding out.

Sapphire sucked the end of her pen.

'I asked Al if he wanted to come but he said

he'd rather watch it on his own. Who would you like to invite?'

Topaz thought for a moment. Her mum would be out in the evening, cleaning offices in East Starbridge. She couldn't invite the others in her class. There was the slim possibility that Miss Diamond wouldn't watch *Murder Mile* but if she invited the others, Miss D would definitely find out. *Someone* would tell her. She would have liked to invite Pearl Wong, but Pearl was in rehearsals for a Christmas Show and anyway, *she* might tell Miss Diamond. If Topaz invited Janice Stone, Kylie Slate might gatecrash the party. Perhaps she could invite Zelma and force her to hand over a cheque the moment the show was on TV.

'I can't think of anyone,' said Topaz. 'Just you, me and Ruby.'

'Is that all?' Ruby asked. 'Isn't there *anyone* else?'

A smile crept across Topaz's face. 'We could send an invitation to the gruesome twosome. That would be so funny. I bet Mrs Quaver will never forgive me for taking Octavia's part as well as my own!'

'But she might turn up,' said Ruby. 'Just to annoy you.'

'So that's it then,' said Sapphire, looking at the piece of paper. 'Our guest list is you, me, Ruby, Nanny Bean, and, if she can be bothered to turn up, my mother. That doesn't seem enough for a party. How

105

about a sleepover instead? Parks can run us to school next day.'

Topaz could hardly concentrate for the next week. She wanted to go up to her classmates and say, 'Next Thursday evening I'm on prime-time television. I'm playing two parts!' She *particularly* wanted to go up to Jasper Pretty and tell him. He'd been annoying her with his crowing about being the Ice Prince in the Ice Spectacular. She'd have *loved* to have gone up to Amber Morelli and told her, but Amber would definitely have run straight to Miss Diamond.

So instead, she sat in class, secretly practising her autograph, dreaming of what her life would be like *after* the TV show. People would stop her on the street and say, 'You were marvellous! What a star!' The nasty Starbridge High girls they'd met in Grease Galore would be glad that they'd asked for her autograph. Perhaps *Snapped!* would run a photo-spread: *A Day in the Life of Topaz L'Amour*. Zelma Flint's phone would be ringing off the hook with offers of work. Zelma would pay her and then she'd be able to buy a new school blazer. Would she even *need* a new blazer? Perhaps she would be offered so many parts she'd have to have a private tutor to school her on film sets or in television studios. Perhaps she would be so famous they'd make an exception for her and she wouldn't need to have lessons, *ever again*. *Murder Mile* was definitely going to be the start of a glittering show business career!

'Look at the size of those!' gasped Topaz, as Parks the chauffeur pulled up in front of two enormous wrought-iron gates, tipped with gold.

A small brass plaque announced: *Starbridge Hill Hall*.

Quietly, smoothly, the gates swung open, and Parks drove through, the gravel on the drive crunching under the car tyres. Topaz craned her neck to get a glimpse of the house, but the tall green hedges flanking either side of the driveway blocked her view.

As the car rounded a corner, ahead of them was a pretty stone house.

'There!' Topaz whispered to Ruby as they approached it. 'Isn't it lovely?'

Topaz went to undo her seat belt, but instead of stopping, the car drove on.

'Have we gone past?' asked Topaz, looking back at the house as they took a left where the driveway forked.

Parks shook his head. 'No, Miss Topaz. That's where *I* live. This is where Miss Stratton lives.'

Ruby and Topaz stared open-mouthed at the house in front of them as the car purred to a halt. Surrounded by jewel-green lawns was an enormous pale grey stone house, each window bordered by white wooden shutters. Over the large front door a stone canopy was perched on slender grey columns of marble. Starbridge Hill Hall looked like a perfect life-sized doll's house.

Topaz scrambled out on to the creamy-coloured gravel as Parks got their bags out of the car and took them into the house.

'Hi!'

Sapphire appeared, blowing her nose.

'Everything all right?' asked Topaz, noticing Sapphire had pink eyes and a blotchy face as if she had been crying.

'Mum isn't coming,' Sapphire sniffed. 'I hadn't heard from her so I rang Rupert about half an hour ago.'

'But she promised to come to the party!' said Topaz, feeling terrible for Sapphire. 'What was her excuse?'

'She said that she promised to come to a *party*, and as we're not having a proper one, there was no point in coming back from wherever she went to.' Sapphire blew her nose again. 'I don't think she ever intended to come.'

Ruby and Topaz exchanged despairing glances. Vanessa Stratton might be a wonderful film star, but she wasn't a wonderful mother.

'What a fantastic place to live,' said Ruby, as Sapphire led them around the side of the house.

'You've got tennis courts!' gasped Topaz, looking around her. 'Proper tennis courts with no weeds or graffiti or broken nets!'

'I never use them,' said Sapphire. 'I just hit a ball against the garage.'

'You mean you've got an entire tennis court and you just use the garage wall?' asked Ruby incredulously.

Sapphire shrugged. 'I've got no one to play with. Nanny Bean is always worried her artificial hip is going to pop out of place if she does any exercise.'

'You are *so* lucky to live here,' said Topaz, thinking of the tiny top-floor flat she shared with her mother.

'Am I?' Sapphire asked. 'I find it embarrassing. That's why I've never invited you here. I mean, how many rooms do you need?'

'How many have you got?' asked Topaz.

'I'm not sure,' said Sapphire. 'I'll give you a tour and you can count.'

It wasn't long before Topaz lost track of the number of rooms Sapphire showed them as they wandered through the vast house, up stairs, down stairs, through large landings and tiny corridors. There was an inner hall and an outer hall, a West Hall and an East Hall, a kitchen and a breakfast room, a room just to do the laundry, a conservatory next to what Sapphire called a drawing room and another room which looked almost the same but which was a lounge with a summer room. There was a dining room which looked as if it was never used, lots of doors which Sapphire pointed to and said were storerooms, bedrooms and bathrooms galore, an office for Sapphire's father, even though he was never at home to use it, and even a room which Sapphire said was just for her mum's shoes.

'Just shoes?' asked Topaz.

'And boots,' said Sapphire, opening the door to a room which was lined with footwear of every colour and heel height.

Vanessa Stratton's shoe room is bigger than my bedroom! thought Topaz as Sapphire closed the door behind them and they clattered back down the stairs and along more corridors. Sapphire's bedroom was huge, with matching furniture, thick cream carpet, pale yellow curtains and yellow and white bedding, but there were no posters on the walls, photographs stuck to a mirror or soft toys lined up on the bed. It was like the rest of the house, beautiful and stylish, but strangely unloved and unlived in.

'Do you have a swimming pool?' asked Ruby.

Sapphire nodded and led them down another corridor.

There was something very eerie about being in a huge room with a swimming pool that had no one swimming in it. The only sound was the gentle hum of the water filter and an overhead fan.

'How often do you use it?' asked Ruby, remembering the unused tennis courts.

'I can't remember the last time I was in here,' said Sapphire, bending down and running her hands through the water. 'I'm not allowed to swim on my own and it's no fun just swimming up and down with Nanny Bean watching me.'

She looked at her watch. 'It's nearly time for the programme! We'll watch it in here.'

Sapphire opened a door leading off the corridor. 'Mum calls it her screening room.'

Topaz couldn't believe her eyes when she stepped into the room. It wasn't just that the room resembled a mini-cinema, with a large screen on one wall and row upon row of plush pink velvet seats, it was the fact that Sapphire had decorated the room with balloons and banners and streamers. One of the chairs had balloons tied to it and a cushion embroidered with *Queen of the Screen*.

'That's Mum's,' said Sapphire as Topaz picked it up. 'But I thought you should have it.'

Topaz gave Sapphire a hug.

'This is so fantastic, Sapphy,' she said. 'I can't believe what you've done. It's one of the nicest things anyone has *ever* done for me.'

The door opened and a small woman carrying a pair of knitting needles, a ball of wool and a huge bowl of popcorn walked in.

'This is Nanny Bean,' said Sapphire, taking the bowl of popcorn. 'She looks after me when Mum and Dad are away, which is all the time.'

Nanny Bean nodded, gave a tight-lipped smile, sat down at the back of the room and began knitting.

Ruby and Sapphire sat on either side of Topaz in her decorated chair. Sapphire pointed the remote control towards the screen and it burst into life. The medical soap opera *Blood, Bleeps and Bandages* was coming to an end. It was strange to see a TV programme on such a large screen, and Topaz felt slightly nervous at the prospect of seeing her face blown up to such huge proportions.

'It's a shame Al isn't here,' said Ruby, dipping her hand into the popcorn. 'Even though he didn't say anything, I know he was excited.'

'If it's a success it could relaunch his career,' said Topaz, thinking to herself, *and launch mine.*

In the flat above the café, Al settled down with a cappuccino and a plate of egg and chips.

This is probably the last night I can do this, he thought, allowing himself a smug smile. From now on he'd be in demand, just as he was all those years ago when he'd first played Inspector 'Nosey' Parker. This time, he had it all worked out. The special would be a huge success and Petunia Bluff at Prism Television would offer him a new series. He'd have his old table back at top celebrity restaurant, the Truffle Pig, perhaps even buy a new red sports car. He'd keep the café but let Topaz's mum run it. Offers of work would flood in and Zelma Flint would *beg* to be his agent again, but he'd take great delight in refusing to return her phone calls.

Yeah! Al the star is back in town, he thought to himself as he popped another chip into his mouth.

'Look!' cried Ruby. 'It's about to start.'

The three girls stared at the television.

Nanny Bean continued to knit.

Topaz felt she was about to burst with excitement. Here she was, sitting in a

beautiful house with a bowl of popcorn, her two best friends beside her, and she was about to star on television.

Life doesn't get much better than this! she thought, clutching her *Queen of the Screen* cushion.

Suddenly the giant screen turned black and the word *Newsflash* appeared in white.

A solemn voice announced, 'We interrupt this programme to bring you a newsflash. Over live to the Pulsar News studio and our newsreader, Dan McMaster.'

'What's happening?' cried Topaz, panic-stricken. 'Where's my programme?'

A stern-faced Dan McMaster appeared on the screen.

'A government spokesman has just announced the resignation of the Prime Minister after he was charged earlier this evening with shoplifting a large-sized bottle of Lush Locks 4 Men hair restorer from a branch of Wellington's the Chemist. In this special edition of *Pulsar News Nightly*, we look back on the career of the follicularly challenged Prime Minister and ask, would wearing a toupee have saved his career? The Christmas special of *Murder Mile* will be shown some time next year.'

There was total silence in the room, then the tip-tap of Nanny Bean's knitting needles started again.

Sapphire switched the television off. The air was thick with disappointment. Even the balloons seemed to shrivel before their eyes. Topaz stared at the blank screen as her dreams of stardom came crashing down around her. The Prime Minister's shoplifting was a disastrophe for *both* their careers.

'At least it solves the problem of what to tell Miss Diamond,' said Ruby, gently patting Topaz's arm.

'It *will* be shown,' said Sapphire. 'We'll keep an eye out for the listings.'

Nanny Bean stopped knitting. 'It won't be shown this Christmas as they'll have their schedule already in place,' she said, giving a gummy smile. 'They'll show it during the summer when no one will want to watch a Christmas special.'

And with that, Topaz buried her head in her *Queen of the Screen* cushion and burst into tears.

In his flat above the café, Al switched off the television, wiped away a tear with a tea towel and went downstairs. It was dark except for the glow from the streetlights outside. He picked up a paper napkin, scribbled on it and stuck it on the door with a blob of marmalade.

Chapter Eleven

'Are you OK?' asked Ruby when she saw Sapphire ambling along the corridor towards the second-year locker rooms, a frown etched across her face.

'Not really,' she replied. 'I'm *really* worried about Topaz. She hasn't been herself since *Murder Mile* was cancelled. And she was bitterly disappointed to have to give up being a snowflake. Has she even said whether she's going to be in the audience for the show tomorrow night?'

Ruby shook her head. She'd hardly seen anything of Topaz since the night of the disastrous screening at Starbridge Hill Hall.

'Haven't you just had jazz dance with her?' she asked. 'Didn't you see her then?'

'Yes,' Sapphire nodded. 'But she shot out the door the moment Anton finished teaching.' Her frown grew deeper. 'It's just not like her. I usually have to drag her out of the studio to stop her standing in front of the mirror.'

'Next time I see her I'm going to ask her what's wrong,' said Ruby. 'She must know we care— Argh!'

Topaz came careering out of the locker room and smacked straight into Ruby who doubled up in pain, the sheet music she was carrying fluttering to the ground.

'Sorry, Rubes!' gasped Topaz, scuttling around trying to pick up the scattered music. She thrust it into Ruby's hand and, calling, 'See you tomorrow!' over her shoulder, began to race down the corridor.

'Hang on a minute.' Sapphire darted after her. 'How about we go for a hot chocolate or something? We haven't done that for a while.'

Topaz paused for a moment. 'But Al's is still closed!'

'There are other cafés in Starbridge, you know. We could go somewhere else.'

'But we like Al's. And look what happened when we went to Grease Galore,' said Topaz, shuffling from one foot to the other and jiggling anxiously on the spot.

'We don't know when Al's is going to reopen so it's about time we found somewhere else,' persisted

Sapphire as Ruby caught up with them. 'Let's go and look for one now.'

A look of panic crossed Topaz's face.

'I can't,' she said. 'Sorry, but I'm in a rush.'

Ruby looked at her friend suspiciously. 'Are you *sure* there isn't something wrong? You're always rushing off after school, we never seem to see you . . .'

'I'm fine, I'm fine,' Topaz interrupted, clearly agitated and desperate to leave.

'Well, what are you up to now?' asked Ruby. 'What's so bad you can't tell us?'

Both friends noticed a slight flush creep up Topaz's neck.

'I'm just going home, that's all,' she said. 'I'll see you tomorrow.' And with that, she was off.

'There's *definitely* something she's not telling us,' said Sapphire as they walked out of school. 'Did you see the look on her face when she said she was going home? She's up to something, I'm sure of it. But what?'

'Without the ice show and now the TV show is cancelled, I *bet* she's got Zelma Flint to get her another part,' said Ruby. 'She'll have gone back and asked to audition for the Raspberry Rumble campaign or that computer shipwreck programme and she doesn't want to tell us.' Ruby gave a disapproving look. 'Telling fibs to us is one thing, but when Miss D finds out, she'll go bonkers.'

Sapphire felt hurt to think Topaz wouldn't tell her the truth.

'Perhaps she really *is* going home,' she said. 'Perhaps she just doesn't want to be friends with us any more. Perhaps now she's seen where I live she feels she can't be friends with me.'

'Topaz wouldn't be like that,' said Ruby. 'There's got to be something else and we'll ask her again tomorrow. Let's go back to the East Wing and watch TV in the common room. *Proof of the Pudding* will be on soon.'

Sapphire gave Ruby a weak smile. 'OK, but just let me go and tell Parks to pick me up later. You go on ahead and I'll catch you up.'

Ruby headed off and Sapphire walked down the steps of the school, along Stellar Terrace and round the corner into Galaxy Street where Parks was waiting in the car. Although Sapphire had finally admitted to her friends that a chauffeur wearing a peaked cap ferried her to and from school every day, she couldn't quite bring herself to let the rest of the school know, and so still made Parks wait around the corner.

She rapped on the glass. Parks wound down the window.

'I'm going to stay at Ruby's for a bit,' she said.

'Can I ring you later so you can come and collect me?'

'Miss Topaz didn't want to join you then?' said Parks, beginning to start the engine.

'She had to rush home,' said Sapphire.

'I've just seen her waiting to get on a bus into town,' said Parks. 'She was at the bus stop when I drove round the corner.'

'Are you sure?' asked Sapphire. 'She said she was going home, but that would mean a bus in the opposite direction.'

Parks nodded. 'Quite sure. I thought it odd that she was going into town on her own as the three of you always do everything together. She had to wait a while for a bus, because look, it's only just pulled away.' He nodded towards the end of the road as a bus belched out black smoke, heading towards town.

'Quick!' shouted Sapphire, jumping into the front seat next to a startled Parks. 'Follow that bus!'

'But what about Miss Ruby?' said Parks as he pressed the accelerator and they shot out into the traffic. 'Aren't you supposed to be seeing her?'

'Just drive!' snapped Sapphire, shocked at how like her mother she sounded. 'Ruby will understand.'

Parks tried his best to keep up with the bus, but despite the fact that it kept pulling in to bus stops, the bus lanes meant it could sail past the queuing traffic and into the distance, leaving Parks and Sapphire trailing behind.

'I'd lose my licence and be out of a job,' Parks said when Sapphire pleaded with him to use the bus lanes. 'Why don't you just ask your friend where she's going instead of following her?'

Because for some reason she won't tell me the truth! thought Sapphire.

In the distance the bus pulled in and a single passenger got out. The bus stop was too far ahead to make out anyone's features, but the passenger was clearly wearing a weird jacket with odd-coloured arms, one of which was much shorter than the other.

'She's there!' cried Sapphire. 'She's just got off the bus. I recognize her blazer.'

'I don't know what she's doing getting off there,' said Parks, looking puzzled. 'There aren't any shops or anything. Just the ice rink.'

Sapphire sat at the edge of the rink and watched as Topaz carefully slid out on to the ice and then confidently began to skate. Sapphire couldn't believe this was the same girl who only a few weeks ago could barely put one skate in front of the other without crashing on to the ice. She'd obviously been practising very hard.

'Hello, Topaz. What are you doing here?' Sapphire called out as Topaz skated towards her.

The sound of Sapphire's voice startled Topaz and she clung to the barrier before making her way off the ice and on to the rubber matting.

'Practising for tomorrow night,' she said, avoiding Sapphire's gaze and unlacing her skates. 'How did you know I was here?'

'Parks saw you getting on the bus and we followed you,' said Sapphire. 'Ruby and I thought you'd pulled out of the show.'

'I was going to,' said Topaz. 'But then *Murder Mile* was cancelled and I changed my mind. I'm going to skate in the show tomorrow.'

'Topaz, don't!' cried Sapphire. 'Look what happened when you tried to practise before. You were so stiff you couldn't even dance. That's why you got into such trouble with Anton and Miss D.'

Topaz shrugged. 'I've been practising for a couple of weeks,' she said. 'Little by little so I didn't get stiff. I'm never going to be a great skater, but at least I can skate well enough to be a snowflake.' She looked at Sapphire's astonished face. 'I've been coming every day after school before the private lessons start.'

'But why didn't you tell me and Ruby?' asked Sapphire.

Sapphire looked hurt and Topaz felt terrible. The

last thing she had wanted to do was upset her friends. She'd kept her skating sessions secret to protect them.

'I'm sorry. I thought if you and Ruby knew, and Miss Diamond knew you knew, you'd get into trouble when Miss D watches the ice show and sees me.' Topaz gulped. 'Everyone says I attract trouble and I didn't want to get you involved.'

'*Please* don't perform tomorrow,' Sapphire pleaded. 'It's not worth losing your scholarship for a few moments under the spotlight.'

Topaz sighed and threw her skates over her shoulder.

'I have to, Sapphy. This is my *only* chance of performing all term, that's why I've been practising so hard. I thought things would happen after *Murder Mile* but now it's cancelled they're not going to. Octavia will be going to auditions and castings whilst I'm stuck at school. I'm getting left behind. I *have* to take any chance to perform, whatever Miss Diamond thinks.'

Topaz began to leave the rink.

'But what about me?' Sapphire yelled out after her. 'What about what *I* think?'

Topaz turned round. Sapphire looked really upset.

'I don't know why you are so against me doing this,' Topaz said. 'It's not *you* who would have to leave Precious Gems. It's me who would be affected.'

'Don't you see?' said Sapphire, tears running down her hot cheeks. 'If you left, however much we promised we'd see each other, we'd grow apart. I just couldn't bear it if you left. You, your mum and Ruby are like family to me. Please, Topaz, don't get into any more trouble!'

Chapter Twelve

Just thinking about what Sapphire had said brought a lump to Topaz's throat and tears to her eyes. Sapphire had looked embarrassed when they'd met at school the next day, but neither of them had said anything about Sapphire's outburst, and Topaz had rushed out of school and got a bus to the rink rather than wait for Sapphire to offer her a lift to the performance.

Perhaps I shouldn't do this after all, thought Topaz, wriggling into her costume: a long white dress and a tiara, which looked silver, but was cheap plastic and scratched her head.

But as she stepped into the main arena so that Boris could give them their final instructions, any thoughts of pulling out of the show vanished.

The rink, which during the day was nothing more than a giant warehouse filled with ice, had been transformed into a magical winter wonderland. Huge ice sculptures of angels and winged horses about to take flight stood dotted between fir trees iced with fake snow and strung with fairy lights. Coloured beams of light pulsated across the ice, as professional skaters in fabulous costumes went through their warm-up routines. In one corner, Octavia and Jasper were tracing moves on the ice. Octavia was wearing a snowflake costume, but instead of a scratchy plastic tiara, she wore a shimmering silver mask and a crown dripping with glittering crystal drops.

The skaters left the rink, the doors opened and the audience began to take their seats, chattering excitedly. The music started, the lights dimmed and the audience gasped as a group of skaters dressed in red and silver dashed on to the rink and skated round at speed, spraying ice all over a surprised but delighted front row of the audience. The show was underway and it was *every* bit as spectacular as the posters had promised! Just as one scene finished, another started, leaving the audience gasping in awe and wanting more. On and on the show went until, finally, Jasper and Octavia skated out into the centre of the rink, bathed in a soft white spotlight as the Ice Prince and Princess began their duet on ice.

The Ice Prince believed he had fallen in love with a humble snowflake – someone his father, the Ice King, would never let him marry – unaware that behind the mask the lowly snowflake was really the rich Ice Princess testing the prince to see whether it was her or her wealth he had fallen in love with. The audience sat dreamy-eyed as Jasper and Octavia performed a ballet on ice.

Boris signalled for the snowflakes to assemble by the sleigh, which was hidden from the audience by a row of fir trees.

Topaz peered at the audience between the scenery. She saw her mother, Lola, in the crowd, sitting next to Ruby and Ruby's father. Professor Rodney Ruddle had paid for her mother's ticket, as promised, to thank her for taking Ruby on holiday. Vanessa Stratton hadn't turned up, but Nanny Bean was in the audience, knitting and watching the show at the same time. Miss Diamond was there, sitting a little too near Amber

Morelli for Topaz's liking. In the front row, with a camera round his neck and a pencil tucked behind his ear, sat Tom 'Scoop' Mackenzie, the show business reporter from *The Starbridge Gazette*. She was surprised to see a group of girls from Starbridge High, still in their uniforms, in the audience. Topaz's heart leapt when she saw one of them was Janice Stone. She remembered when she and Janice had once been best friends, spending hours gossiping, listening to music in each other's bedrooms, window-shopping in Starbridge, taking funny pictures in photo booths and texting each other constantly. Even though they'd promised to stay friends, when Topaz won a place at stage school their lives had gone in different directions and they barely saw each other. Would it be like that with Ruby and Sapphire if she had to leave Precious Gems, and would it be worth it for a few moments in front of an audience and under a spotlight? Scoop Mackenzie's article about the ice show would be fish and chip paper within days, the ice sculptures would have melted, the fir trees and the fairy lights would be moved on to another town. Her moment in the spotlight would be fleeting but the repercussions of performing without the school's permission could last for ever.

What am *I doing?* thought Topaz. *How can I risk not just my scholarship but my friends, just to be one snowflake in a blizzard? There have been enough disastrophes this term already!*

Scurrying out of the line-up of snowflakes, she found Sapphire who was at the back.

'I'm pulling out,' she said. 'I can't do this. I can't risk losing my friends and my scholarship, just to be a snowflake for a couple of minutes.'

'What?' gasped Sapphire. 'It's too late! You can't pull out now! The show must go on!'

Topaz shook her head. 'No, I've made up my mind. I'll pretend I've twisted my ankle at the last minute. As soon as Boris appears I'll tell him.'

There was a commotion as Octavia Quaver burst through the line of fir trees, growling, 'That wretched Pretty boy is *deliberately* trying to steal my limelight! He's trying to upstage me!' She ripped off her mask and tossed it angrily on to the ice. Seeing Topaz, she ordered, 'Pick that up!'

'Pick it up yourself!' Topaz snapped back.

Boris Petrova appeared carrying Octavia's costume for the final scene, a huge silver cape trimmed with white fake fur.

'What is happening?' he demanded.

'Mr Petrova, I'm sorry but I—' Topaz began, heading towards the ice impresario. But as she did so, she caught one of her skates in Octavia's discarded mask and crashed on to the ice with a sickening thud.

'I think I've twisted my ankle,' she groaned,

genuinely in pain. 'Maybe even broken it! I can't stand up!'

Boris was beside himself and began pacing up and down shrieking, 'We can not go on with ninety-nine snowflakes. The symmetry will be ruined!'

'Oh, no one will notice,' snapped Octavia dismissively. 'Who cares about one stupid snowflake?'

Boris's face darkened. 'You wretched girl! This is the Dance of One Hundred Snowflakes!' he roared. 'Not ninety-nine. I've worked on this show for twenty years! Someone in the audience will count the snowflakes and if there is one missing,' he looked shocked, 'my credibility will be in tatters!' He looked at Topaz who was now on her feet leaning against the side of the silver sleigh, rubbing her ankle. 'How did this happen?' he barked.

Before Topaz could speak, Sapphire stepped forward holding Octavia's mask. 'Your Ice Princess threw this down and Topaz tripped over it. It wasn't her fault. It was hers.' She pointed towards a pouting Octavia.

In the background they could hear Jasper's solo coming to an end.

'You!' he snapped, lunging at Octavia and ripping the glittering crown from her head, '*you* are going to be the hundredth snowflake and you . . .' he grabbed a startled Topaz and bundled her into the sleigh, tossing the silver cape, mask and crown in after her, 'you can sit in the sleigh with an injured ankle. You can be the Ice Princess.'

'But *I'm* your Ice Princess,' whined Octavia. 'I can't just be a snowflake. I've had private lessons! I wore a mask! No one will know I skated the duet. I'm not doing it. I'm going to find my mum. She won't let you force me to be a stupid snowflake.'

Boris looked at Octavia menacingly. 'If you ever want to work in this town again, get on to the ice and skate NOW!'

As the Ice Prince finished his solo, the audience clapped and cheered and then gasped with delight as a magnificent silver sleigh surrounded by a hundred snowflakes slid gracefully on to the rink and stopped under the spotlight. The Ice Prince looked distraught. In the sleigh was the masked Ice Princess his father was forcing him to marry, even though he'd fallen in love with the simple snowflake he'd skated with earlier. He'd tried to put the snowflake out of his mind but it was no good! He couldn't go through with the marriage when he loved someone else. He approached the sleigh, miming that he would not be marrying the rich Ice Princess and was turning his back on money for his love.

The snowflakes clustered round the sleigh, the lights

dimmed to a single brilliant spotlight, the music reached a deafening crescendo and the Ice Princess ripped off her mask with a flourish.

'Hello, Jasper!' Topaz whispered as Jasper Pretty fainted and landed in a crumpled heap on the ice.

The snowflakes quivered with panic as, from behind a fir tree, Boris could be heard shrieking, 'Somebody *do* something!'

Topaz looked over the side of the sleigh at Jasper lying on the ice and hissed to the surrounding snowflakes, 'Get him into the sleigh.'

Somehow, the snowflakes managed to haul him to his feet and bundle him over the edge of the sleigh where Topaz dragged him on to the seat next to her.

Jasper was beginning to come round, but still looked dazed and confused. The lights went out and the audience, unaware that Boris's Grand Finale had ended in disaster, clapped and cheered furiously. The lights came on, and the other skaters came out on to the rink and skated round several times to wild applause whilst Topaz sat in the sleigh waving at the audience, some of whom were throwing flowers on to the rink.

All too quickly the sleigh was pulled back behind the fir trees where Boris was waiting, staring into space, a strange look on his face.

'Who was responsible for what happened out there?' he asked, looking at the snowflakes. 'Whose idea was it to drag that wretched boy into the sleigh?'

'Hers!' Octavia shrieked, pointing at Topaz. 'She told the snowflakes to do it. I didn't want to. *She's* the one who ruined your finale, Mr Petrova!'

Boris looked up at Topaz who was still sitting in the sleigh. 'Is this true?' he demanded.

Topaz gulped and nodded.

'See!' crowed Octavia. 'I told you she'd ruined it.'

'Ruined it!' boomed Boris. 'Ruined it! Shut up, you silly girl. It was fantastic! The prince overcome with emotion when he sees his true love! The princess so desperate for the prince she drags him into her sleigh! What drama! What emotion! What an ending!'

'But what was she doing in the sleigh in the first place?' Miss Diamond pushed her way between the snowflakes and stared at Topaz.

'Madam, who are you?' asked Boris, puffing his chest out.

'I'm the Headmistress of Precious Gems Stage School and I'm wondering why one of my pupils is sitting in that sleigh when she knows she's not supposed to.'

Topaz felt her head swim. She had dreaded this moment. The moment when she would be told to leave Precious Gems. And Miss Diamond was about to tell her to leave in front of *everybody*, including Octavia Quaver!

Here we go, she thought, bracing herself.

'She wasn't supposed to be in the sleigh,' Boris said. 'I pushed her in at the last moment and threw the props in after her. Thank goodness I did. She saved the performance!'

'Oh, I see,' said Miss Diamond, looking surprised. She turned to Topaz. 'I'm sorry. For one moment I thought you'd gone behind my back and entered the ice show.'

Topaz pulled her knees up so that the Headmistress wouldn't see she had tights and skates on beneath her cape.

'Go behind your back, Miss Diamond?' said Topaz, pretending to look hurt. 'As if I'd do that!'

Topaz Steals the Show
by Helen Bailey

Topaz L'Amour is ecstatic – she's won a place at Precious Gems Stage School! But in the world of show business, learning to tap dance on the bathroom floor with drawing pins in your trainers counts for nothing. Topaz quickly learns that life at stage school is hard work.

And she doesn't just have to cope with lack of training. Her rival, the scheming and ambitious Octavia Quaver from Rhapsody's Theatre Academy, is doing her best to steal the limelight . . .

Another sparkling Topaz production!

Topaz Takes a Chance
by Helen Bailey

Flushed with her success in the Starbridge
Christmas show, Topaz asks Adelaide Diamond,
Headmistress of Precious Gems, if she can appear
in advertisements. And she's about to audition for
her first big break: the key role in the Zit Stop!
advertising campaign.

But the path to fame and fortune is never smooth –
particularly when blocked by arch-rival Octavia
Quaver from Rhapsody's Theatre Academy . . .

Another sparkling Topaz production!

Topaz in the Limelight
by Helen Bailey

Topaz is in her element at Precious Gems – she knows she's destined to become a star! So when she has a chance encounter with Madame Catovia, a fortune teller at the Starbridge Summer Festival, she ignores the prediction that she will never be a star.

But when her breakthrough part in a film ends up featuring only her left elbow, despite standing next to the poisonous Octavia Quaver during filming – and when she only manages to get a part as a dead body in a re-make of *Murder Mile*, Topaz begins to wonder if Madame Catovia is right after all . . .